Lope de Vega's

FUENTE OVEJUNA

Translation and Introduction by

William E. Colford

Professor, Romance Languages
City College of the City University of New York

Barron's Educational Series, Inc.

Woodbury, New York • London • Toronto • Sydney

FOR MY SON, CHRISTOPHER

PUBLISHER'S FOREWORD

⚜

THIS BILINGUAL EDITION has been prepared with several groups of readers in mind. Like all the Barron Classics in Translation, this volume's primary purpose is to present to the mature student of Comparative Literature a faithful English rendering of a masterpiece of world letters. If he has forgotten much of the Spanish he once studied, he may wish to refresh his knowledge as he reads along; for this purpose the left-hand pages will be helpful, so that he can compare Lope's play with a verse translation that conveys to the English-speaking mind what the original means—and how it sounds—to the Spanish-speaking mind.

Another group consists of English-speaking students of the Spanish language and literature. Now on an advanced level (since they are reading a classic of the Golden Age), such students will focus their attention upon the Spanish pages. An occasional glance at the English version will suffice to clarify any doubts about the meaning of certain seventeenth-century Spanish words, or to confirm the student's remembrance of constructions already learned; it will also help him to grasp quickly the meaning of new expressions, thus dispensing with much time-consuming fingerwork in a detailed end vocabulary, no longer needed at this level of attainment. Linguistic differences—mostly orthographic—between the older Spanish and modern usage are clarified in notes on the same page where they occur. These arrangements will encourage rapid reading by eliminating the need to break the train of thought, as must inevitably occur when the student is forced to turn endlessly back and forth in the book and to thumb through pages of notes and columns of words. After all, the object is to improve his language skills, not his manual dexterity.

A third group consists of the growing number of Spanish-speaking people who are studying English on an advanced, adult level. This group will concentrate on the right-hand pages, with an occasional reference to Lope's original in case of language difficulties.

Finally, it is hoped that all advanced students of Spanish and of English will profit by using this volume as an introduction to the technique of verse translation.

INTRODUCTION

M{ADRID}, 1562. Philip II, austere and pious monarch, has recently ascended the throne relinquished by his famous father Charles V, grandson of Ferdinand and Isabella. Spain, fast approaching the peak of her power, dominates Europe and the New World, and administrative control of her vast empire is now centralized in this fast-growing city to which Philip has just moved the seat of government. It replaces the medieval and Renaissance capitals, which shifted as the reconquest of Spain's territory from the Moors continued; Toledo, Burgos and Valladolid have been relegated to permanent provincial status. High in the heartland of Castile, Madrid stands as the symbol of rising Hispanic power, for its elevation and central location enable it to look down and around at the whole Iberian peninsula—even at Portugal, which Philip will soon absorb, together with that nation's far-flung possessions in America, Africa and the Orient.

Madrid, 1562. The new capital is teeming with administrators needed to direct the affairs of empire, and with the government personnel required to carry on the huge amount of paperwork this entails. Retired or temporarily inactive soldiers, returned from campaigns abroad or awaiting new assignments, mingle with courtiers and courtesans, aristocrats and actors, poets and playwrights, rogues and churchmen, orphaned waifs and religious mystics, the newly rich and the permanently poor. In this Madrid, in this year, Lope de Vega is born, and the bustling, restless life of the swarming city will stimulate the precocious boy destined to become the founder of the Spanish national theater.

At the age of five—before he could even write—Lope would give part of his lunch to schoolboys in exchange for their copying down his poetry as he dictated it. At ten he translated a Latin poem into Spanish verse, and by the time he was twelve he had written his first play, also in verse. In our preoccupation with Lope as a playwright, we should never lose sight of the fact that he is one of the greatest Spanish poets of all time; indeed, with Góngora and Quevedo he forms the great poetic triumvirate of Spain's Golden Age. (Lope, incidentally, opposed Góngora's obscure, over-decorative baroque verse style—called *Culteranismo*—which creeps into Calderón's plays at times.) As early as 1585, when Lope was only twenty-three, Cervantes mentioned him among the outstanding poets of the day. And within three years Lope was also Spain's most popular and celebrated playwright.

It was in this same year of 1588 that Lope went through one of the most turbulent periods of his long and agitated life. He had recently broken with Elena Osorio, a married actress with whom he had formed a liaison when he was a seventeen-year-old theology student at Alcalá. He then ran off with another girl, Isabel de Urbina, but when he left her and joined the Spanish Armada, she married him by proxy. Later that year, upon his return from the disastrous naval expedition, Lope set up their home in Valencia. (He had been exiled from Madrid for eight years by court ruling because of his libelous satires against Elena Osorio and her family. In his defense it might be said that he had become completely disenchanted with her because of her newly-formed relationship with a young nobleman, nephew of a Cardinal.) From Valencia and later from other cities Lope continued to write for the Madrid stage.

After his wife's death ten years later, he was remarried, this time to Juana de Guardo, daughter of a rich meat merchant in Madrid. But he soon fell in love with another actress, Micaela Luján, who became his mistress and bore him five children. After his second wife's death in 1614, Lope became a priest, but still he could not resist women. After at least three more affairs, he took a married woman, Marta de Nevares, to live with him in 1616. Ironic retribution was to come, however, for Doña Marta went blind, then mad, and finally died in 1632. Lope was left with only his dearly cherished daughter Clara, the fruit of his last love, to look after him; but she ran off with a young nobleman who enjoyed the king's protection. Lope's life had come full circle, and he drained the bitter cup during his final years. Almost all of his dozen children—legitimate and illegitimate—had died, including his favorite son, who was drowned en route to the New World in 1634.

But Lope was just as passionate in religion as in love. Believing firmly in his ultimate pardon, he was deeply penitent and flagellated himself cruelly; a whip was found in the room where he died the next year, and there were bloodstains on the walls. Death finally overtook him as the result of a chill contracted while tending his beloved garden.

Literally, all Madrid attended Lope's funeral, for he had been more than a national figure: he was *the* national figure. For almost half a century he had been pointed out to visitors in Madrid as if he were some public monument; in fact, people used to come to Madrid just to see with their own eyes that there actually was a prodigious being who could write so many excellent plays! He far outshone Cervantes in popular esteem all during their overlapping lifetimes: Cervantes lived from 1547 to 1616, and Lope from 1562 to 1635.

Lope had earned about half a million dollars by his literary efforts, but spent freely, gave alms and costly gifts impulsively, and bought expensive art on a lavish scale. Indeed, to emphasize the cost or excellence of any item, the people of Madrid coined a phrase that passed into the language: "es de Lope." Almost his entire fortune had been dissipated by the time he died.

Such are the tragic highlights of the personal life of Lope Félix de Vega Carpio. Despite two complicated marriages (he sometimes had two homes simultaneously), three all-consuming love affairs, and innumerable passing romantic entanglements, he managed to take part in two military campaigns (one against the Azores and one as a member of the Armada), to conduct a voluminous correspondence as secretary to four noblemen, to devote much time to charitable and religious duties, to travel frequently, to write novels and other prose works as well as heroic narrative poems and a huge outpouring of lyric poetry, and to compose—

by Lope's own count—1500 plays. He wrote literally millions of lines, most of them in verse—virtually a whole literature. Of his plays (some biographers mention as many as 1800 or 2000) only 470 have come down to us, but we know the titles of at least 300 more. He was a man simply brimming over and bursting with vitality, who lived dynamically and loved life intensely.

Not a moment of his long literary life was wasted. Even as a young recruit aboard the galleon *San Juan* in the Spanish Armada, Lope wrote most of the twenty cantos of his long heroic poem *La hermosura de Angélica*, a continuation of Ariosto's *Orlando furioso*. And at the other end of his life, almost his last literary effort was a revision of his youthful work *La Dorotea*, an autobiographical novel in dialogue form that deals with his first love affair, the one with Elena Osorio. What memories of a long and lusty life must have crowded into his mind as the septuagenarian completed this revision in 1632!

Lope apparently placed little permanent value upon his plays, perhaps because he dashed them off so hurriedly. Because of the insatiable demand of the Spanish public for theatrical works, which ran for only a few days, Lope turned out two plays a week regularly for many years; and he tells us that more than a hundred of his plays were written in a single day each! "If anyone should criticize my plays," he says, "and think that I wrote them for fame, disabuse him of this and tell him that I wrote them for money." Obviously, Lope lacked the time to polish his plays; but the majestic sweep of his lyric lines and the sheer beauty of his verse—which welled up within him and gushed forth as from a deep, abundant spring—make many of his plays masterpieces of world literature. In Spanish letters only Cervantes surpasses Lope in depth, but no one excels him in creative force.

The student of Comparative Literature should note that the two truly national theaters of the sixteenth and seventeenth centuries were the English and the Spanish. The French was more limited in its appeal at that time, catering as it did to the upper bourgeoisie and the aristocracy. In both Spain and England it was the theater of all the people. Shakespeare (1564–1616) was a complete contemporary of Lope de Vega, and their respective roles in literature are the same: each is his nation's theatrical genius. Each came into prominence about 1590, Lope slightly ahead of Shakespeare. And each took the burgeoning theater of his day and molded it into the form it was to follow thereafter.

Except for the fact that women acted on the stage in Spain, the theaters in the two countries were remarkably alike, even in physical appearance. The open-roofed Globe in London was similar to the open courtyards between houses that served as theaters in Madrid and other Spanish cities. The first permanent playhouses were opened in Madrid about 1570, and were rather primitive by later standards. When the Teatro del Príncipe and the Teatro de la Cruz were built, they remained the only public theaters in the whole city until late into the eighteenth century. It was within the physical limitations of such simple playhouses (much like our present-day "theater in the round") that Lope had to work. And both in England and in Spain the "groundlings" occupied a prominent place—figuratively as well as literally—because Shakespeare and Lope took the reactions of the general public into careful consideration.

Just as Cervantes combined all the earlier types of Spanish prose narrative and gave definitive form to the modern Spanish novel, so did Lope de Vega fuse all the earlier efforts of the Spanish stage into a truly national theater. He even wrote a verse treatise called *Arte nuevo de hacer comedias en este tiempo* (1609) as a summary of his new technique. (The word "comedia" had come to mean any full-length secular play.) Lope's "new style of writing plays" greatly modified or deliberately disregarded the three classic unities of time, place and action. "When I set out to write a play," Lope tells us, "I lock up all the rules with six sets of keys." He reduced the number of acts from five to three, with a rapid dénouement at the very end of the third act, and created for the Spanish people the kind of dashing drama they wanted, and which fitted this era in their history. His genius touched all types of plays—historical, religious and romantic. Lope thus set the guidelines for all subsequent playwrights during the Golden Age, and his influence comes down to this very day.

He captured the spirit of the Spanish nation in his works, which he imbued with all the breadth and vigor of his own personality. His was not a theater for a select minority, but for all the people: at this juncture in their cultural history, he seemed to answer some deep-felt need in Spain's national life.

Lope did not look upon his country with Cervantes' twisted, melancholy smile, or with the ironic bitterness expressed by Quevedo. To be sure, the long afternoon of Spain's declining power had begun with the very disaster in which Lope took part in 1588. (Cervantes had fought in the naval victory of Lepanto in 1571, which marked the high noon of Spanish military prowess.) But twilight is often the most beautiful part of the day, and its glow, reflecting from Lope's many-faceted genius, continued through most of the seventeenth century.

Calderón, who composed about two hundred theatrical pieces (Shakespeare wrote thirty-seven), dealt almost exclusively with the nobility and the aristocracy in his plays; he himself came from a distinguished Madrid family. Lope, who came from humble stock, wrote about all levels of Spanish society, and excelled in plays that depict the peasantry. To understand Calderón's profound and subtle dramas a great deal of philosophical and historical background is necessary; the action is secondary, and the theme is all-important. Lope's action-packed plays are clearly theatrical, and appeal to a larger, more general audience.

We can point definitely to Calderón's *Life is a Dream* as his masterpiece, and to Segismundo as his greatest single character; but when we consider Lope's innumerable theatrical pieces there is no single play or person that stands out above all others. After all, no one work could adequately encompass the genius of Lope de Vega, who was the spokesman for the triumphant spirit of an entire nation. (The same might be said, of course, about Shakespeare: which is his "best" play?) Of the dozen or so of Lope's works generally accorded top ranking by the world's critics, *Fuente Ovejuna* and *Peribáñez y el Comendador de Ocaña*—both of which deal with conflicts between the peasantry and the nobility —are recognized as his best by the vast majority of literary historians. And while *Peribáñez* (the name of the protagonist) depicts the clash between that humble man and the noble Commander of Ocaña, *Fuente Ovejuna* (the name of a town) deals with the collective action of an entire community against their feudal overlord. Hence, the latter gives us a broader sweep of the whole panorama of Spanish society at a critical moment in its development during the Renaissance.

Fuente Ovejuna, in which the action takes place in 1476, is based on historical fact. When Isabella of Castile married Ferdinand of Aragon against the wishes of her brother, King Henry IV ("el Impotente"), the king designated Juana (his presumptive daughter) as next in line of succession. But it was widely believed that Juana was really the child of the queen and a Court favorite, Beltrán de la Cueva. When King Henry died in 1474, the way was open to civil war between the partisans of Isabella and those of "la Beltraneja," as Juana was disrespectfully called. King Alfonso V of Portugal, who had married Juana under such irregular circumstances that the Church refused to recognize their union, supported her claim to the throne. The military-religious Order of Calatrava, which figures prominently in the play, was at first divided over the question. The Grand Master (Don Rodrigo in our play) and the Grand Commander (our Don Fernán, feudal lord of the town of Fuente Ovejuna) sided with Juana against Isabella.

The source material for *Fuente Ovejuna* was readily available to Lope in a work published in 1572, Rades y Andrada's *Crónica de las tres Ordenes Militares*. The three great Spanish Orders referred to were Calatrava, Santiago and Alcántara, all of which were founded in the Middle Ages; they existed well into the twentieth century, and were influential in Spanish political and religious affairs. Moreover, the phrase "Fuente Ovejuna lo hizo" (Fuente Ovejuna did it) had passed into the language, and was commented upon by Covarrubias in his *Tesoro de la lengua castellana*, which appeared in 1611, only a few years before the first printing of Lope's *Fuente Ovejuna* (1619).

Another source, of course, was that storehouse of traditional lore, the popular ballads. The outrages of Commander Don Fernán, especially against the village women, had come down through the centuries in song and story, and appear in our play in the appropriate selection sung by the musicians at the wedding feast (Act II, Scene 16):

> *The maiden goes down to the valley,*
> *With her hair flowing free in the breeze;*

Calatrava's bold knight makes a sally,
And the cross on his doublet she sees.
Among the thick branches she plunges
To conceal her confusion and fear;
The knight through the brush onward lunges,
And she feigns not to see him so near. (etc.)

Lope wove together the historical background and the popular ballads that dealt with the lecherous Commander Don Fernán to form a spirited play of political intrigue, personal passion and collective vengeance that has captured the heart of the Hispanic world on both sides of the Atlantic for the past three and a half centuries. Shakespeare had the same genius for fusing national history and traditional legend, as he did for example in *King Lear* by cleverly combining the sad story of Lear and his three daughters with the tragic tale of the Earl of Gloucester and his two sons.

Because *Fuente Ovejuna* deals with a popular uprising against a feudal overlord it has been considered by some critics a "revolutionary" play. In the 1920's, many performances of Anatole Lunacharsky's Russian rendering were given in towns in the Soviet Union, no doubt because the peasant folk in the play slew their noble master. Actually, Lope had no thought of inciting anyone to rebellion. Quite to the contrary, *Fuente Ovejuna* is studded with passages that extol obedience to constituted authority, particularly to the monarchy. It is in the name of the Catholic Monarchs that the peasants revolt against Don Fernán, who was not only a petty tyrant but also a traitor to the Spanish crown because he favored foreign intervention by the Portuguese against Isabella of Castile. As Spain evolved from the feudal ideas of the Middle Ages toward the more modern Renaissance concept of monarchy during the fifteenth century, the power of the local nobility in many towns and villages was sternly curbed by Ferdinand and Isabella; and this trend was accentuated by their successors, the Hapsburgs, particularly Charles V and Philip II. Lope, who was a man of the people, appreciated the rise of the villagers—farmers and artisans—to a higher status in Spanish life, and celebrated their greater freedom and dignity in many of his plays. This theme—praise for the benign monarch who sides with the people against the nobility—is a favorite of Lope's, and he excelled in plays of this type, the finest example of which is *Fuente Ovejuna*.

The idea that the peasants had no "honor" is frequently expressed by villainous members of the provincial nobility in the classic Spanish theater as justification for their own misdeeds. Lope and the playwrights who followed him distinguished clearly between honor as social standing derived from birth alone and honor as inherent personal and moral integrity possessed by all men regardless of their rank and position in society. In *Fuente Ovejuna* this is clearly brought out in the conflict between the upright farmer-mayor Esteban and the depraved Commander Don Fernán. And while the mayor and the other men of the village are hesitant about rising in revolt, the women seize the initiative under the leadership of the mayor's daughter Laurencia, whose impassioned speech (Act III, Scene 3) finally shames the men into action:

> *And do you call yourselves good, upright men?*
> *Are you my relatives—my father, too—*
> *Who look upon me thus in such travail*
> *And do not burst with grief and righteous wrath?*
> *You are just sheep! The very village name*
> *Of Fuente Ovejuna means "a fount*
> *Where sheep come for a drink"—and such are you!* (etc.)

This action of the women is also true to historical fact, as is the mayor's instruction given to the people to reply simply "Fuente Ovejuna did it" to all questioning later, even under torture. Hence the whole village is the hero of the play, and no one person has the principal role.

This is what makes *Fuente Ovejuna* unique among Lope's plays, and what differentiates it from other dramas of the classic Spanish theater, many of which deal with the all-pervading theme of honor. Here we have a kind of collective honor which Lope cleverly couples with patriotic loyalty to the Catholic Monarchs, Ferdinand and Isabella. Thus, this play epitomizes the deepest feelings of Spaniards of every social level; this includes the nobility, because Don Fernán, in addition to behaving traitorously toward his sovereigns, fails to live up to the code of conduct expected of a nobleman. God, country and honor were tightly woven into the very fabric of Spanish society during the Golden Age.

The best Spanish version of the play is the Aguilar edition by Sainz de Robles (1952), which was used as the basis of this present translation. *Fuente Ovejuna* has also been adapted or translated (principally in prose) in the major European languages, including Polish as well as Russian. Lope uses several rhyme-schemes in it, thus following his own dictum about suiting the verse-form to the action and the speaker; however, the Spanish national meter, the eight-syllable *romance,* takes precedence over other forms. It has been thought best, therefore, to employ the English national verse-form, iambic pentameters, in this translation. As in Lope's play, there are several small sections in other meters where songs and interpolated poems are part of the play; and where Lope uses a sonnet, as in Laurencia's monologue in Act III, Scene 16, we have used a sonnet also. The procedure throughout has been to remain very close to the original, within the framework of English verse. And because two short eight-syllable lines of Lope's play often combine to form one of our longer iambic pentameters, the play in English seems shorter than it is in the original Spanish.

WILLIAM E. COLFORD

New York, 1969

Lope de Vega's FUENTE OVEJUNA

PERSONAS

El Rey Don Fernando
La Reina Doña Isabel
El Maestre de Calatrava
Fernán Gómez

Don Manrique
Esteban, *Alcalde*
Laurencia
Frondoso
Juan Rojo
Alonso, *Alcalde*
Jacinta
Pascuala
Barrildo
Mengo
Ortuño
Flores
Cimbranos, *Soldado*
Leonelo

Un juez, un niño, tres regidores, labradores y labradoras, soldados, músicos, acompañamiento

La acción pasa en Fuente Ovejuna y en otros puntos.

1476

DRAMATIS PERSONAE

King Ferdinand *of Aragon, husband of*
Queen Isabella *of Castile*
Don Rodrigo Téllez Girón, *Master of the Order of Calatrava*
Don Fernán Gómez de Guzmán, *Grand Commander of the Order of Calatrava*
Don Manrique, *Master of the Order of Santiago*
Esteban, *Mayor of Fuente Ovejuna, and father of*
Laurencia, *a peasant girl, bride of*
Frondoso, *a peasant*
Juan Rojo, *a peasant, and uncle of Laurencia*
Alonso, *joint Mayor of Fuente Ovejuna*
Jacinta
Pascuala } *peasant girls*
Barrildo
Mengo } *peasants*
Ortuño
Flores } *servants of Don Fernán*
Cimbranos, *a soldier*
Leonelo, *a law student*

A judge, a boy, aldermen, peasants, soldiers, musicians, attendants

The action takes place in and around Fuente Ovejuna, and elsewhere.

Time: 1476

ACTO PRIMERO

ESCENA 1

Habitación del Maestre de Calatrava en Almagro

Salen el Comendador, Flores y Ortuño

COMENDADOR: ¿Sabe el maestre que estoy
en la villa?
FLORES: Ya lo sabe.
ORTUÑO: Está, con la edad, más grave.

COMENDADOR: Y ¿sabe también que soy
Fernán Gómez de Guzmán?

FLORES: Es muchacho, no te asombre.

COMENDADOR: Cuando no sepa mi nombre
¿no le sabrá el que me dan
de comendador mayor?
ORTUÑO: No falta quien le aconseje
que de ser cortés se aleje.
COMENDADOR: Conquistará poco amor.

ACT ONE

SCENE 1

Home of Don Rodrigo, Master of the Order of Calatrava,
in Almagro

*Enter Fernán Gómez, Commander of the Order,
with Flores and Ortuño*

COMMANDER: The Master knows that I have come to town?

FLORES: He is aware of it, my lord.

ORTUÑO: The lad
  Is older now, and more mature.

COMMANDER: And does
  He realize that I am Don Fernán,
  A Gómez de Guzmán?

FLORES: He's but a boy;
  You should not be surprised if he does not.

COMMANDER: But even though he may not know my name,
  Is not the lad aware, at least, that I
  Hold rank as Grand Commander?

ORTUÑO: There are those
  Who counsel him against such courtesies.

COMMANDER: There's little love that he will win that way,

3

Es llave la cortesía
para abrir la voluntad;
y para la enemistad
la necia descortesía.

ORTUÑO: Si supiese un descortés
cómo lo aborrecen todos
—y querrían de mil modos
poner la boca a sus pies—,
antes que serlo ninguno,
se dejaría morir.

FLORES: ¡Qué cansado es de sufrir!
¡Qué áspero y qué importuno!
Llaman la descortesía
necedad en los iguales,
porque es entre desiguales
linaje de tiranía.
Aquí no te toca nada:
que un muchacho aun no ha llegado
a saber qué es ser amado.

COMENDADOR: La obligación de la espada
que se ciñó, el mismo día
que la cruz de Calatrava
le cubrió el pecho, bastaba
para aprender cortesía.

FLORES: Si te han puesto mal con él,
presto le conocerás.

ORTUÑO: Vuélvete, si en duda estás.

COMENDADOR: Quiero ver lo que hay en él.

ESCENA 2

Sale el Maestre de Calatrava y acompañamiento

MAESTRE: Perdonad, por vida mía,
Fernán Gómez de Guzmán;
que ahora nueva me dan
que en la villa estáis.

For courtesy's the key that wins good will,
While thoughtless lack of it makes enemies.

ORTUÑO: If a discourteous man but knew how all
Despise him and attempt to thwart him in
A thousand ways, he would as lief be dead
As be like that!

FLORES: And what a bore he is!
How coarse, and how uncouth! Discourtesy
Is foolish among those of equal rank,
And tyranny toward those of lesser stamp.
But in this matter here you should not feel
Aggrieved, my lord: it simply means the lad
Has not yet learned the value of respect.

COMMANDER: The very day he girded on his sword,
And had the Cross of Calatrava pinned
Upon his breast, he took upon himself
The obligation to learn courtesy.

FLORES: If they have tried to prejudice the boy
Against you, sire, you soon will find it out.
ORTUÑO: If you have doubts, my lord, then why not leave?
COMMANDER: I fain would see just what the lad is like.

SCENE 2

Enter the young Master of Calatrava, with his retinue

MASTER: Upon my life! Your pardon, Don Fernán.
I have but now received the news that you
Are here in town.

COMENDADOR: Tenía
muy justa queja de vos;
que el amor y la crianza
me daban más confianza,
por ser, cual somos los dos,
vos maestre en Calatrava,
yo vuestro comendador
y muy vuestro servidor.

MAESTRE: Seguro, Fernando, estaba
de vuestra buena venida.
Quiero volveros a dar
los brazos.

COMENDADOR: Debéisme honrar;
que he puesto por vos la vida
entre diferencias tantas,
hasta suplir vuestra edad
el Pontífice.

MAESTRE: Es verdad.
Y por las señales santas
que a los dos cruzan el pecho,
que os lo pago en estimaros
y como a mi padre honraros.

COMENDADOR: De vos estoy satisfecho.

MAESTRE: ¿Qué hay de guerra por allá?

COMENDADOR: Estad atento, y sabréis
la obligación que tenéis.

MAESTRE: Decid que ya lo estoy, ya.

COMENDADOR: Gran maestre, don Rodrigo
Téllez Girón, que a tan alto
lugar os trajo el valor
de aquel vuestro padre claro,
que, de ocho años, en vos
renunció su maestrazgo,

COMMANDER: I have just cause to be
Annoyed. My love for you and my own rank
Had led me to expect more, due to our
Relationship: you are the Master of
Our Order, and in Calatrava I
Am Grand Commander—and your servant, sir.

MASTER: Your welcome here is certain, Don Fernán:
Again I would embrace you with these arms.

COMMANDER: You should indeed pay honor to me, for
I've risked my life quite often for you and
Have had the Pope declare you are of age.

MASTER: That's true; and by our Order's sacred Cross,
Which we both wear upon our breast, I shall
Repay you with esteem and honor you
As if you were my father.

COMMANDER: I am pleased.
MASTER: What tidings from afar about the war?
COMMANDER: Pay heed, and you will know your duty clear.

MASTER: Please speak; I am attending to you now.
COMMANDER: Grand Master Don Rodrigo, you were raised
To your exalted post eight years ago
By your brave father, who renounced his right.

que después por más seguro
juraron y confirmaron
reyes y comendadores,
dando el Pontífice santo
Pío segundo sus bulas
y después las suyas Paulo
para que don Juan Pacheco,
gran maestre de Santiago,
fuese vuestro coadjutor:
ya que es muerto, y que os han dado
el gobierno sólo a vos,
aunque de tan pocos años,
advertid que es honra vuestra
seguir en aqueste caso
la parte de vuestros deudos;
porque, muerto Enrique cuarto,
quieren que al rey don Alonso
de Portugal, que ha heredado,
por su mujer, a Castilla,
obedezcan sus vasallos;
que aunque pretende lo mismo
por Isabel don Fernando,
gran príncipe de Aragón,
no con derecho tan claro
a vuestros deudos, que, en fin,
no presumen que hay engaño
en la sucesión de Juana,
a quien vuestro primo hermano
tiene ahora en su poder.
Y así, vengo a aconsejaros
que juntéis los caballeros
de Calatrava en Almagro,
y a Ciudad Real toméis,
que divide como paso
a Andalucía y Castilla,
para tomarlos a entrambos.

You were confirmed in this by monarchs and
Commanders, and two Holy Fathers—Paul
And Pius Second—issued bulls that named
Don Juan Pacheco, the Grand Master of
Santiago, as coadjutor with you.
Pacheco now is dead, and you alone—
Despite your tender years—command us all.
Now bear in mind that you are honor bound
To all your relatives to take up arms
In their behalf in this dynastic war.
The death of Henry IV[1] has caused your kin
To wish their vassals to support the cause
Of Don Alfonso, King of Portugal,[2]
Who claims Castile as his wife's heritage.
The great Prince Ferdinand of Aragon,
Through Isabella, also has a claim;
Your family feels, however, that his rights
Are not so clear as those of Juana[3] whom
Your cousin now holds in his power. Hence
I come to urge that you convene the Knights
Of Calatrava in Almagro here;
Then capture Ciudad Real, which guards
Both Andalusia and Castile. To take

---

[1] *Henry IV of Castile (1454–1474)*

[2] *Alfonso V (1438–1481)*

[3] *Juana la Beltraneja*

Poca gente es menester,
porque tienen por soldados
solamente sus vecinos
y algunos pocos hidalgos,
que defienden a Isabel
y llaman rey a Fernando.
Será bien que deis asombro,
Rodrigo, aunque niño, a cuantos
dicen que es grande esa cruz
para vuestros hombros flacos.
Mirad los condes de Urueña,
de quien venís, que mostrando
os están desde la tumba
los laureles que ganaron;
los marqueses de Villena,
y otros capitanes, tantos,
que las alas de la fama
apenas pueden llevarlos.
Sacad esa blanca espada,
que habéis de hacer, peleando,
tan roja como la cruz;
porque no podré llamaros
maestre de la cruz roja
que tenéis al pecho, en tanto
que tenéis blanca la espada;
que una al pecho y otra al lado,
entrambas han de ser rojas;
y vos, Girón soberano,
capa del templo inmortal
de vuestros claros pasados.

MAESTRE: Fernán Gómez, estad cierto
que en esta parcialidad,
porque veo que es verdad,
con mis deudos me concierto.

These realms your army need be small: they have
As soldiers just their peasants and a few
Hidalgos—loyal to Isabella—who
Consider Ferdinand their rightful king.
Rodrigo, you are but a lad; this deed
Would dazzle those who say that Cross you wear
Is far too heavy for your youth to bear.
Behold the Counts of Urueña, your
Own ancestors; from out the tomb they come
To show you all the laurels they have won.
Behold the Marquess of Villena and
The many other captains in his train,
Whose throng the wings of fame can scarce sustain.
Now draw your unstained sword, and as a Knight
Of Calatrava plunge into the fray:
Let your bright sword turn scarlet in the fight,
Just like that Cross you wear. Until that day
You cannot call yourself—with any right—
Our Master, nor hold Calatrava's sway;
The sword you bear must be of blood-red hue,
Just like the Cross you wear upon your breast.
Rodrigo, Master, bring new honor to
Your noble forebears' brave, immortal rest!

MASTER: You may be certain, Don Fernán, that I
Am on my family's side in this dispute,
For I can see that they are wholly right.

Y si importa, como paso
Ciudad Real al mi intento,
veréis que como violento
rayo sus muros abraso.
No porque es muerto mi tío
piensen de mis pocos años
los propios y los extraños
que murió con él mi brío.
Sacaré la blanca espada
para que quede su luz
de la color de la cruz,
de roja sangre bañada.
Vos ¿adónde residís?
¿Tenéis algunos soldados?

COMENDADOR: Pocos, pero mis criados,
que si dellos os servís,
pelearán como leones.
Ya veis que en Fuenteovejuna
hay gente humilde, y alguna
no enseñada en escuadrones,
sino en campos y labranzas.

MAESTRE: ¿Allí residís?

COMENDADOR: Allí
de mi encomienda escogí
casa entre aquestas mudanzas.
Vuestra gente se registre;
que no quedará vasallo.

MAESTRE: Hoy me veréis a caballo,
poner la lanza en el ristre.

(*Vanse*)

And if the capture of Ciudad Real
Is needed for this enterprise, you shall
Behold me strike it like a thunderbolt.
I realize that I am young in years,
But let not friend or foe believe that I
Have lost my courage with my uncle's death.
My unstained, shining sword I will unsheathe;
It shall be bathed in blood and made as red
In color as our Cross. But, Don Fernán,
Where do you live? And have you any men?

COMMANDER: Of soldiers I have few; my servants, though,
Will fight like lions if you so command.
In Fuente Ovejuna we have folk
Who are but humble farmers, and more skilled
In agriculture than in arts of war.

MASTER: You live there?

COMMANDER: Yes; I chose a house on lands
I own there, and all through these troubled times
I shall stay on. Call up your knights: let none
Remain behind.

MASTER: This day you will behold
Me armed and mounted on my charger bold.

(Exeunt)

ESCENA 3

Plaza de Fuenteovejuna

Salen Pascuala y Laurencia

LAURENCIA: ¡Mas que nunca acá volviera!

PASCUALA: Pues a la he[1] que pensé
que cuando te lo conté
más pesadumbre te diera.

LAURENCIA: ¡Plega al cielo que jamás
le vea en Fuenteovejuna!

PASCUALA: Yo, Laurencia, he visto alguna
tan brava, y pienso que más;
y tenía el corazón
brando[2] como una manteca.

LAURENCIA: Pues ¿hay encina tan seca
como esta mi condición?

PASCUALA: Anda ya; que nadie diga:
desta agua no beberé.

LAURENCIA: ¡Voto al sol que lo diré,
aunque el mundo me desdiga!
¿A qué efecto fuera bueno
querer a Fernando yo?
¿Casárame con él?

PASCUALA: No.

LAURENCIA: Luego la infamia condeno.
¡Cuántas mozas en la villa,
del Comendador fiadas,
andan ya descalabradas! [3]

PASCUALA: Tendré yo por maravilla
que te escapes de su mano.

[1] *he*   fe

[2] *brando*   blando

[3] *descalabradas*   deshonradas

SCENE 3

The village square in Fuente Ovejuna

Enter Laurencia and Pascuala

LAURENCIA: Oh, would that he might never more return!

PASCUALA: In faith, I thought you would be more distressed
    When I informed you that he'd left.

LAURENCIA: God grant
    That I may never see that man again
    In Fuente Ovejuna!

PASCUALA: I have seen
    Some girls, Laurencia, firm as you—and more—
    Yet underneath, their hearts were butter-soft.

LAURENCIA: Is there an oak that's harder than my will?

PASCUALA: Be careful: no one can be certain that
    He'll never thirst for water.

LAURENCIA: Well, I can,
    Although the world may say it is not so.
    What good would it do me to love Fernán?
    Do you believe that I would marry him?

PASCUALA: Of course not.

LAURENCIA: I denounce his perfidy.
    Too many village maidens here have placed
    Their trust in the Commander and have found
    Themselves betrayed.

PASCUALA: I shall consider it
    A miracle if you escape his toils.

LAURENCIA: Pues en vano es lo que ves
porque ha que me sigue un mes,
y todo, Pascuala, en vano.
Aquel Flores, su alcahuete,
y Ortuño, aquel socarrón,
me mostraron un jubón,
una sarta y un copete.
Dijéronme tantas cosas
de Fernando, su señor,
que me pusieron temor;
mas no serán poderosas
para contrastar mi pecho.

PASCUALA: ¿Dónde te hablaron?

LAURENCIA: Allá
en el arroyo, hoy habrá
seis días.

PASCUALA: Y yo sospecho
que te han de engañar, Laurencia.

LAURENCIA: ¿A mí?

PASCUALA: Que no, sino al cura.

LAURENCIA: Soy, aunque polla, muy dura
yo para su reverencia.
Pardiez, más precio poner,
Pascuala, de madrugada,
un pedazo de lunada
al huego[1] para comer,
con tanto zalacatón
de una rosca que yo amaso,
y hurtar a mi madre un vaso
del pegado cangilón,
y más precio al mediodía
ver la vaca entre las coles
haciendo mil caracoles
con espumosa armonía;

---

[1] *huego*   fuego

LAURENCIA: What you have seen this month is all in vain,
   Pascuala, all in vain. That Flores man,
   His go-between, and that Ortuño fool
   Have been pursuing me, and showing me
   A blouse, a necklace, and a headdress, too.
   They said so many things about Fernán,
   Their master, that I am afraid of him;
   But things like that can never win my heart.

PASCUALA: Where was it that they spoke to you?
LAURENCIA: Down there,
   Beside the brook, about six days ago.

PASCUALA: Laurencia, I suspect you'll be deceived.

LAURENCIA: Who, me?
PASCUALA: I don't exactly mean the priest!
LAURENCIA: I may be just a little chicken, but
   I'm tough: His Highness will not relish me!
   Pascuala, I would rather put a piece
   Of bacon on the fire each day at dawn,
   And eat it with a twist of homemade bread
   And wash it down with wine I've taken from
   My mother's jug; and then at noon I would
   Prefer to see boiled beef and cabbage all
   A-bubbling and a-whirling as they cook;

y concertar, si el camino
me ha llegado a causar pena,
casar una berenjena
con otro tanto tocino;
y después un pasatarde,
mientras la cena se aliña,
de una cuerda de mi viña,
que Dios de pedrisco guarde;
y cenar un salpicón
con su aceite y su pimienta,
e irme a la cama contenta,
y al "inducas tentatión" [1]
rezarle mis devociones,
que cuantas raposerías,
con su amor y sus porfías,
tienen estos bellacones;
porque todo su cuidado,
después de darnos disgusto,
es anochecer con gusto
y amanecer con enfado.

PASCUALA: Tienes, Laurencia, razón;
que en dejando de querer,
más ingratos suelen ser
que al villano el gorrión.
En el invierno, que el frío
tiene los campos helados,
descienden de los tejados,
diciéndole "tío, tío",
hasta llegar a comer
las migajas de la mesa;
mas luego que el frío cesa,
y el campo ven florecer,
no bajan diciendo "tío",
del beneficio olvidados,
mas saltando en los tejados
dicen: "judío, judío".

[1] *"Et ne nos inducas in tentationem."*   The Lord's Prayer

And if I'm tired at journey's end I'd like
To blend a piece of eggplant with salt pork;
And then a snack, while supper's being fixed:
A bunch of grapes just picked right off my vines
(May God protect them from all harm by hail);
And then to sup on peppers with chopped meat
And oil. Then off to bed I go content,
With first my little prayer of "Lead us not
Into temptation . . ." All of this, I say,
Is better than the tricks of some base knave.
For men all plead their love, but what they crave
Is pleasure when they go to bed, and then
Next day they make life hard for us again.

PASCUALA: Laurencia, you are right; for when they tire
Of loving us they're more ungrateful than
The sparrows are to farmers: in the cold
Of winter when the fields are frozen fast
The birds swoop from the roof and start to chirp
"Sweet, sweet!" And then they even hop upon
The table and pick up the crumbs to eat.
But when the cold abates and sparrows see
The fields begin to bloom, they do not come
And say "Sweet, sweet!" but fly up to the roof,
Forgetting bounties past, and cry "Cheap, cheap!"

Pues tales los hombres son:
cuando nos han menester,
somos su vida, su ser,
su alma, su corazón;
pero pasadas las ascuas,
las tías somos judías,
y en vez de llamarnos tías,
anda el nombre de las pascuas[1].

LAURENCIA: No fiarse de ninguno.

PASCUALA: Lo mismo digo, Laurencia.

ESCENA 4

Salen Mengo, Barrildo y Frondoso

FRONDOSO: En aquesta diferencia
andas, Barrildo, importuno.

BARRILDO: A lo menos aquí está
quien nos dirá lo más cierto.

MENGO: Pues hagamos un concierto
antes que lleguéis allá,
y es, que si juzgan por mí,
me dé cada cual la prenda,
precio de aquesta contienda.

BARRILDO: Desde aquí digo que sí.
Mas si pierdes ¿que darás?

MENGO: Daré mi rabel de boj,
que vale más que una troj,
porque yo le estimo en más.

BARRILDO: Soy contento.

FRONDOSO: Pues lleguemos.
Dios os guarde, hermosas damas.

LAURENCIA: ¿Damas, Frondoso, nos llamas?

---

[1] *El nombre de las pascuas*   prostitutas

Well, that is how men are: when they have need
Of us we are their life, their heart, their soul,
Their all; but when their ardor cools we are
Not "Sweet!" but "Cheap!". Our bounties past they have
Forgotten, and they call us nasty names.

LAURENCIA: Trust none of them; you'll have yourself to blame.

PASCUALA: Laurencia, you are right; I say the same.

SCENE 4

Enter Mengo, Barrildo and Frondoso

FRONDOSO: Barrildo, you are wrong in this dispute.

BARRILDO: At any rate, here's someone who will tell
Us what is right.

MENGO: But let it be agreed,
Before you reach them, that each one of you
Will pay the bet to me if I am right.

BARRILDO: Agreed! But if you lose, what will you give?

MENGO: My boxwood flute, which is worth more to me
Than any granary.

BARRILDO: I'm satisfied.

FRONDOSO: Then let's approach. Good morrow, ladies fair.

LAURENCIA: My dear Frondoso! "Ladies," did you say?

FRONDOSO: Andar al uso queremos:
al bachiller, licenciado;
al ciego, tuerto; al bisojo,
bizco; resentido, al cojo,
y buen hombre, al descuidado.
Al ignorante, sesudo;
al mal galán, soldadesca;
a la boca grande, fresca,
y al ojo pequeño, agudo.
Al pleitista, diligente;
gracioso, al entrometido,
al hablador, entendido,
y al insufrible, valiente.
Al cobarde, para poco;
al atrevido, bizarro;
compañero, al que es un jarro,
y desenfadado, al loco.
Gravedad, al descontento;
a la calva, autoridad;
donaire, a la necedad,
y al pie grande, buen cimiento.
Al buboso, resfriado;
comedido, al arrogante;
al ingenioso, constante;
al corcovado, cargado.
Esto al llamaros imito,
damas, sin pasar de aquí;
porque fuera hablar así
proceder en infinito.

LAURENCIA: Allá en la ciudad, Frondoso,
llámase por cortesía
desa suerte; y a fe mía,
que hay otro más riguroso
y peor vocabulario
en las lenguas descorteses.

FRONDOSO: Querría que lo dijeses.

LAURENCIA: Es todo a esotro contrario:
al hombre grave, enfadoso;

FRONDOSO: We wish to ape the fashion of the day:
  A college boy is called "professor" and
  A blind man has a "visual defect."
  A man who's cross-eyed has a "roving glance;"
  A crippled man is said to "limp a bit;"
  A spendthrift's praised for "liberality;"
  A tongue-tied fool's the "smart-but-silent type;"
  A braggart's liked as "brave and soldierly!"
  A large mouth means a person's "generous;"
  A beady eye denotes a man who's "shrewd;"
  A man who's always suing in the courts
  "Upholds the law;" a gossip is a "wit;"
  Glib talkers are "such sympathetic folks,"
  And bores are classified as "eloquent."
  A coward's just "a quiet sort" at heart;
  The brash and thrusting fellow's called "gallant;"
  A drunkard is "a gay companion," and
  A lunatic is thought "a little queer."
  The chronic grumbler is "the earnest type;"
  The bald man has "a brave and noble brow,"
  And foolish talk's confused with "sprightly wit."
  The big-shoed man "has both feet on the ground;"
  The man with pox but "suffers from a cold;"
  The arrogant are often called "polite,"
  And shifty men are thought of as "quite firm,"
  While hunchbacks simply "have a lot to bear."
  And so I ape the fashion of the day
  And call you "ladies;" but I shall desist
  Lest I enumerate an endless list.

LAURENCIA: That kind of talk may pass for courtesy
  In cities; but, Frondoso, by my faith,
  Our rustic tongues use harder words than those.

FRONDOSO: I'd love to hear a sample of your style.

LAURENCIA: It's quite the opposite of yours. We call
  A serious-minded man "a grumpy bore,"

al que es veraz, descompuesto;
melancólico, al compuesto,
y al que reprehende, odioso.
Importuno, al que aconseja;
al liberal, moscatel;
al justiciero, crüel,
y al que es piadoso, madeja.
Al que es constante, villano;
al que es cortés, lisonjero;
hipócrita al limosnero,
y pretendiente, al cristiano.
Al justo mérito, dicha;
a la verdad, imprudencia;
cobardía, a la paciencia,
y culpa, a lo que es desdicha.
Necia, a la mujer honesta;
mal hecha, a la hermosa y casta,
y a la honrada . . . Pero basta;

MENGO: Digo que eres el dimuño[1].

BARRILDO: ¡Soncas que lo dice mal![2]

MENGO: Apostaré que la sal
la echó el cura con el puño.

LAURENCIA: ¿Qué contienda os ha traído,
si no es que mal lo entendí?

FRONDOSO: Oye, por tu vida.

LAURENCIA: Di.

FRONDOSO: Préstame, Laurencia, oído.

LAURENCIA: Como prestado, y aun dado,
desde ahora os doy el mío.

FRONDOSO: En tu discreción confío.

LAURENCIA: ¿Qué es lo que habéis apostado?

FRONDOSO: Yo y Barrildo contra Mengo.

---

[1] *dimuño*   demonio
[2] *Soncas*   ciertamente

And one who speaks the truth is "so uncouth;"
An even-tempered man is labelled "sad,"
And one who disapproves is "full of spite."
A "busybody" is the name we give
To one who tries to offer good advice,
While one who helps his friends just "interferes."
To mete out justice is to be "too cruel,"
But if you're merciful they call you "weak."
The steady-minded man is called "so dull;"
Politeness is considered "flattery;"
A charitable man's a "hypocrite;"
A pious Christian goes to church "for show."
A well-deserved reward is "just good luck;"
The truthful man's considered "quite unwise,"
And patience is a sign of "cowardice."
Misfortune means "he got his just deserts;"
A faithful wife is thought of as a "fool;"
A pretty girl who's chaste has "something wrong;"
An honest woman is . . . But why should I
Go on? I've said sufficient in reply.

MENGO: You are the very devil, I declare!

BARRILDO: Not badly put!

MENGO: I'll bet the priest poured on
The salt in fistfuls when he christened her!

LAURENCIA: But what is this dispute that brought you here—
Unless I have misunderstood your words?

FRONDOSO: Now listen very carefully.

LAURENCIA: Go on.

FRONDOSO: Laurencia, kindly lend your ear to me.

LAURENCIA: Just lend? I'll give it to you now, for keeps!

FRONDOSO: I trust your judgment.

LAURENCIA: What's the bet about?

FRONDOSO: We've made a bet, Barrildo here and I,
Against friend Mengo.

LAURENCIA: ¿Qué dice Mengo?

BARRILDO: Una cosa
  que, siendo cierta y forzosa,
  la niega.

MENGO: A negarla vengo,
  porque yo sé que es verdad.

LAURENCIA: ¿Qué dice?

BARRILDO: Que no hay amor.

LAURENCIA: Generalmente, es rigor.

BARRILDO: Es rigor y es necedad.
  Sin amor, no se pudiera
  ni aun el mundo conservar.

MENGO: Yo no sé filosofar;
  leer ¡ojalá supiera!
  Pero si los elementos
  en discordia eterna viven,
  y de los mismos reciben
  nuestros cuerpos alimentos,
  cólera y melancolía,
  flema y sangre, claro está.

BARRILDO: El mundo de acá y de allá,
  Mengo, todo es armonía.
  Armonía es puro amor,
  porque el amor es concierto.

MENGO: Del natural os advierto
  que yo no niego el valor.
  Amor hay, y el que entre sí
  gobierna todas las cosas,
  correspondencias forzosas
  de cuanto se mira aquí;
  y yo jamás he negado
  que cada cual tiene amor,
  correspondiente a su humor,
  que le conserva en su estado.
  Mi mano al golpe que viene
  mi cara defenderá;

LAURENCIA: What does he contend?

BARRILDO: Well, he denies a fact that's clear and plain.

MENGO: I do, because I know I speak the truth.

LAURENCIA: What does he say?

BARRILDO: That love does not exist.

LAURENCIA: It does, of course.

BARRILDO: Of course it does, the fool!
  Without it, this whole world could not go on.

MENGO: I cannot spin philosophy with you,
  And as for reading—how I wish I could!
  But I contend that Nature's elements
  Are in eternal discord, and since we
  Receive our nutriments from them, it's clear
  Our bodies must absorb their wrath and phlegm
  And sorrows and dislikes along with them.

BARRILDO: This world—and worlds beyond—Mengo, my friend,
  Is naught but harmony. And harmony's
  Pure love, for love is perfect harmony.

MENGO: I don't deny the value of self-love:
  I must admit that love like that exists;
  Perforce it governs the relationships
  Among all things we see upon this earth.
  I never have denied that everyone
  Has love befitting his own state in life:
  Self-preservation is at stake in this.
  My hand defends my face from any blow;

mi pie, huyendo, estorbará
el daño que el cuerpo tiene.
Cerraránse mis pestañas
si al ojo le viene mal,
porque es amor natural.

PASCUALA: Pues ¿de qué nos desengañas?

MENGO: De que nadie tiene amor
más que a su misma persona.

PASCUALA: Tú mientes, Mengo, y perdona;
porque, ¿es materia el rigor
con que un hombre a una mujer
o un animal quiere y ama
su semejante?

MENGO: Eso llama
amor propio, y no querer.
¿Qué es amor?

LAURENCIA: Es un desco
de hermosura.

MENGO: Esa hermosura
¿por qué el amor la procura?

LAURENCIA: Para gozarla.

MENGO: Eso creo.
Pues ese gusto que intenta
¿no es para él mismo?

LAURENCIA: Es así.

MENGO: Luego ¿por quererse a sí
busca el bien que le contenta?

LAURENCIA: Es verdad.

MENGO: Pues dese modo
no hay amor sino el que digo,
que por mi gusto le sigo
y quiero dármele en todo.

BARRILDO: Dijo el cura del lugar
cierto día en el sermón
que había cierto Platón
que nos enseñaba a amar;

My feet, by running, will ward off all hurt
That might befall my body; and my eyes
Will blink their lashes to protect my sight,
For this is Nature's love of self—and right.

PASCUALA: Then what is it you wish to prove to us?
MENGO: That man has love for no one but himself.

PASCUALA: Forgive me, but I must say that's not true.
Do you think that man's love for woman's false?
And do not all the animals need mates?

MENGO: I call that love of self, and not true love.
What is this thing that you call love, I ask?

LAURENCIA: The search for what is beautiful in life.

MENGO: And why does love seek what is beautiful?

LAURENCIA: In order to enjoy it.
MENGO: I believe
That, too. And this enjoyment which it seeks
Is for itself—or am I wrong?
LAURENCIA: You're right.
MENGO: Then, through self-love it seeks what gives it joy?

LAURENCIA: That's true.
MENGO: If that be so, there is no love
Except the kind I speak about—the kind
That I pursue to give me every joy.

BARRILDO: The village curate said the other day,
When he was preaching, that there was a man
Called Plato who had taught about his love—

que éste amaba el alma sola
y la virtud de lo amado.

PASCUALA: En materia habéis entrado
que, por ventura, acrisola
los caletres de los sabios
en sus cademias[1] y escuelas.

LAURENCIA: Muy bien dice, y no te muelas
en persuadir sus agravios.
Da gracias, Mengo, a los cielos,
que te hicieron sin amor.

MENGO: ¿Amas tú?

LAURENCIA: Mi propio honor.

FRONDOSO: Dios te castigue con celos.

BARRILDO: ¿Quién gana?

PASCUALA: Con la quistión[2]
podéis ir al sacristán,
porque él o el cura os darán
bastante satisfacción.
Laurencia no quiere bien,
yo tengo poca experiencia.
¿Como daremos sentencia?

FRONDOSO: ¿Qué mayor que ese desdén?

ESCENA 5

Sale Flores

FLORES: Dios guarde a la buena gente.

PASCUALA: Este es del Comendador
criado.

LAURENCIA: ¡Gentil azor!
¿De adónde bueno, pariente?

---

[1] *cademias*   academias

[2] *quistión*   cuestión

The love of virtue and the soul alone.

PASCUALA: Now there you've raised a question that perhaps
  Professors in academies and schools
  Are racking their inquiring brains to solve.

LAURENCIA: She's right. Now, Mengo, don't exhaust yourself
  Attempting to convince her; just give thanks
  To Heaven that it made you free of love!

MENGO: Are you in love?
LAURENCIA: I love my honor, yes.
FRONDOSO: For that, may God smite you with jealousy!
BARRILDO: Now tell us: Who has won the argument?
PASCUALA: For answer to that question you should see
  The priest or else the sacristan, for they
  Alone can best reply. Laurencia here
  Is not involved too deeply, and I've had
  But scant experience with love. How can
  We render judgment? Hence, we shall refrain.

FRONDOSO: What greater judgment than your cold disdain?

SCENE 5

Enter Flores

FLORES: May God be with all good folk such as you.
PASCUALA: (This fellow is the Grand Commander's page.)

LAURENCIA: (His heathen bird of prey!) Whence come you,
  friend?

FLORES: ¿No me veis a lo soldado?

LAURENCIA: ¿Viene don Fernando acá?

FLORES: La guerra se acaba ya,
   puesto que[1] nos ha costado
   alguna sangre y amigos.

FRONDOSO: Contadnos cómo pasó.

FLORES: ¿Quién lo dirá como yo,
   siendo mis ojos testigos?
   Para emprender la jornada
   desta ciudad, que ya tiene
   nombre de Ciudad Real,
   juntó el gallardo maestre
   dos mil lucidos infantes
   de sus vasallos valientes,
   y trescientos de a caballo
   de seglares y de freiles[2],
   porque la cruz roja obliga
   cuantos al pecho la tienen,
   aunque sean de orden sacro;
   mas contra moros, se entiende.
   Salió el muchacho bizarro
   con una casaca verde,
   bordada de cifras de oro,
   que sólo los brazaletes
   por las mangas descubría,
   que seis alamares prende.
   En un bridón corpulento,
   rucio rodado, que al Betis
   bebió el agua, y en su orilla
   despuntó la grama fértil;
   el codón labrado en cintas
   de ante, y el rizo copete
   cogido en blancas lazadas,
   que con las moscas de nieve

---

[1] *puesto que*　aunque

[2] *freiles*　frailes

FLORES: But don't you see me dressed in uniform?

LAURENCIA: Is Don Fernán returning also, then?

FLORES: The war is over, but we've spilt some blood
And lost some friends.

FRONDOSO: Please tell us what took place.

FLORES: Who better can relate the tale than I,
Whose eyes were witnesses to everything?
To undertake the capture of the town
Named Ciudad Real, the valiant Don
Rodrigo raised two thousand gallant men
On foot, selected from his vassals bold.
He also raised three hundred mounted men,
Some laymen and some friars: the red Cross
We wear upon our breast obliges all
To battle, those in holy orders, too—
But just against the Moors, you understand.
The youthful Master wore a doublet green
With gilded border seen between the slits
The sleeves had in them, fastened by six clasps.
He rode astride a barrel-chested steed,
A dapple-gray from Andalusia's plains,
That had imbibed the waters of its streams
And grazed the pastures on their fertile banks.
Its tail was twined with buckskin plaits behind;
Its rippling mane, in front, was tied with bows
That vied in whiteness with the flakes of snow

que bañan la blanca piel
iguales labores teje.
A su lado Fernán Gómez,
nuestro señor, en un fuerte
melado, de negros cabos,
puesto que con blanco bebe.
Sobre turca jacerina,
peto y espaldar luciente,
con naranjada orla saca,
que de oro y perlas guarnece.
El morrïón, que corona
con blancas plumas, parece
que del color naranjado
aquellos azahares vierte;
ceñida al brazo una liga
roja y blanca, con que mueve
un fresno entero por lanza,
que hasta en Granada le temen.
La ciudad se puso en arma;
dicen que salir no quieren
de la corona real,
y el patrimonio defiende.
Entróle bien resistida,
y el maestre a los rebeldes
y a los que entonces trataron
su honor injuriosamente
mandó cortar las cabezas,
y a los de la baja plebe,
con mordazas en la boca,
azotar públicamente.
Queda en ella tan temido
y tan amado, que creen
que quien en tan pocos años
pelea, castiga y vence,
ha de ser en otra edad
rayo del Africa fértil,
que tantas lunas azules
a su roja cruz sujete.

That seemed to fleck its iridescent flanks.
Our own lord Don Fernán rode right along
Beside him on a honey-colored mount
Whose fetlocks, mane and nose were black as jet,
Except for whitish foam about its mouth.
He wore a coat of mail of Turkish make
With orange-colored trimmings, all bedecked
With gold and pearls upon the shining plates
Of steel protecting both his chest and back;
And on his head a helmet crowned with plumes
Of white, like orange blossoms that spilled down
Cascading from its orange-colored trim.
His ashwood lance—a veritable tree
That rested on his arm supported by
A white and scarlet brace—struck fear into
The Moors of old Granada far away.
The city rushed to arms, and all proclaimed
Reluctance to renounce the royal crown.
They battled to defend their heritage,
But after strong resistance we marched in.
Our Master ordered all the rebel chiefs
And those who had besmirched his honor then
To be beheaded. Commoners who fought
Were gagged and flogged right in the public square.
He made himself so greatly feared—and yet
Respected—in the town that those who saw
The youth wage war and win, and castigate
His enemies, predicted that he would
Grow up to be the scourge of all Islam
In fertile Africa, and would subject
Their crescent blue to his bright scarlet Cross.

Al Comendador y a todos
ha hecho tantas mercedes,
que el saco de la ciudad
el de su hacienda parece.
Mas ya la música suena:
recibidle alegremente,
que al triunfo las voluntades
son los mejores laureles.

ESCENA 6

Salen el Comendador y Ortuño, Juan Rojo,
Esteban y Alonso; músicos, labradores

MÚSICOS (*Cantan*):   *Sea bien venido*
el Comendadore
de rendir las tierras
y matar los hombres.
¡Vivan los Guzmanes!
¡Vivan los Girones!
Si en las paces blando,
dulce en las razones.
Venciendo moriscos,
fuertes como un roble,
de Ciudad Reale
viene vencedore;
que a Fuenteovejuna
trae sus pendones.
¡Viva muchos años,
viva Fernán Gómez!

COMENDADOR: Villa, yo os agradezco justamente
el amor que me habéis aquí mostrado.

ALONSO: Aun no muestra una parte del que siente.
Pero ¿qué mucho que seáis amado,
mereciéndolo vos?

He seized so much and gave it to his men
And to our own Commander that it seemed
As if he were disbursing many gifts
From his estate instead of from a town
That he had sacked. But music now I hear:
Give joyful welcome to his mighty sword,
For good will is the victor's best reward.

SCENE 6

*Enter the Commander, Juan Rojo, Esteban, Alonso
and Ortuño, with musicians and peasants*

MUSICIANS (*singing*)
     We welcome you, Commander,
     Returning with your band,
     For you have slaughtered many men
     And captured Moorish land.

     Long live the name Guzmán!
     Long live the name Girón!
     Their hearts, while soft in times of peace,
     When fighting Moors are stone.

     To Fuente Ovejuna
     From Ciudad Real
     He brings triumphant banners home:
     Long live our Don Fernán!

COMMANDER: Good townfolk, let me thank you now, I pray,
     For all the love you've shown me here today.

ALONSO: Of what it feels the town shows but a part:
     You merit love from each and every heart.

ESTEBAN: Fuenteovejuna
   y el regimiento[1] que hoy habéis honrado,
   que recibáis os ruega y importuna
   un pequeño presente, que esos carros
   traen, señor, no sin vergüenza alguna,
   de voluntades y árboles bizarros,
   más que de ricos dones. Lo primero
   traen dos cestas de polidos barros;
   de gansos viene un ganadillo entero,
   que sacan por las redes las cabezas,
   para cantar vueso[2] valor guerrero.
   Diez cebones en sal, valientes piezas,
   sin otras menudencias y cecinas,
   y más que guantes de ámbar, sus cortezas.
   Cien pares de capones y gallinas,
   que han dejado vïudos a sus gallos
   en las aldeas que miráis vecinas.
   Acá no tienen armas ni caballos,
   no jaeces bordados de oro puro,
   si no es oro el amor de los vasallos.
   Y porque digo puro, os aseguro
   que vienen doce cueros, que aun en cueros
   por enero podréis guardar un muro,
   si dellos aforráis vuestros guerreros,
   mejor que de las armas aceradas;
   que el vino suele dar lindos aceros.
   De quesos y otras cosas no excusadas
   no quiero daros cuenta: justo pecho
   de voluntades que tenéis ganadas;
   y a vos y a vuestra casa, buen provecho.
COMENDADOR: Estoy muy agradecido.
   Id, regimiento, en buena hora.
ALONSO: Descansad, señor, ahora,
   y seáis muy bien venido;

---

[1] *regimiento*   Concejo Municipal

[2] *vueso*   vuestro

ESTEBAN: The burgesses and council of this town
  Of Fuente Ovejuna, honored here
  By you today, request (but not without
  Some shame) that you accept our humble gifts.
  Behold the rustic presents in these carts:
  They are not rich, but come straight from our hearts.
  The first contains two baskets loaded with
  Glazed earthenware; next comes a flock of geese
  Whose cackling heads out through these crates proclaim
  Your martial valor; then ten salted hogs,
  Prize animals, and other products made
  Of pork; then sides of beef with glist'ning hides
  So smooth they seem like softest, scented gloves;
  A hundred brace of capon and some hens
  That left their roosters widowers in towns
  You passed nearby. Out here we have no arms
  Or horses' trappings of pure gold for you:
  The only gold is your true vassals' love.
  And speaking now of purity, here's wine—
  Yes, twelve great skins of it—which, if it lined
  Your soldiers' skins inside could hold the line
  Against the foe in January's cold
  Much better than their arms sharp-edged with steel,
  For wine will put an edge on arms and men.
  These are but tokens of esteem, and hence
  I do not list the cheeses and the rest:
  May you and yours with love and health be blessed.

COMMANDER: I thank you from the bottom of my heart;
  Dear councilmen, in peace may you depart.
ALONSO: Please rest now, sire; you are most welcome here.

que esta espadaña que veis
y juncia a vuestros umbrales
fueran perlas orientales,
y mucho más merecéis,
a ser posible a la villa.

COMENDADOR: Así lo creo, señores.
Id con Dios.

ESTEBAN: Ea, cantores,
vaya otra vez la letrilla.

MÚSICOS (*Cantan*): *Sea bien venido*
el Comendadore
de rendir las tierras
y matar los hombres.

(*Vanse los Alcaldes, labradores y músicos*)

ESCENA 7

El Comendador, Laurencia, Pascuala, Ortuño, Flores

COMENDADOR: Esperad vosotras dos.

LAURENCIA: ¿Qué manda su señoría?

COMENDADOR: ¡Desdenes el otro día,
pues, conmigo! ¡Bien, por Dios!

LAURENCIA: ¿Habla contigo, Pascuala?

PASCUALA: Conmigo no, tirte afuera.

COMENDADOR: Con vos hablo, hermosa fiera,
y con esotra zagala.
¿Mías no sois?

PASCUALA: Sí, señor;
mas no para cosas tales.

COMENDADOR: Entrad, pasad los umbrales;
hombres hay, no hayáis temor.

We wish that these rude rushes spread upon
Your threshold as a sign of homage were
Rich oriental pearls, for you deserve
Much more if we could but afford such gifts.

COMMANDER: I thank you kindly. Goodbye, gentlemen.

ESTEBAN: Come, singers, let us hear your song again.

MUSICIANS (*singing*)
             We welcome you, Commander,
             Returning with your band,
             For you have slaughtered many men
             And captured Moorish land . . .

           (*Exeunt Musicians, Peasants and Councilmen*)

SCENE 7

Laurencia and Pascuala start to leave

COMMANDER: Now you two girls stay here.

LAURENCIA: What is it, sire?

COMMANDER: The other day you scorned me. Me, no less!

LAURENCIA: Pascuala, is it you he means?

PASCUALA: Not me!
  Just leave me out of this!

COMMANDER: I'm speaking now
  To you, my pretty wildcat; also to
  This other country wench. Are you not mine?

PASCUALA: We are your vassals, sire, but that is all.

COMMANDER: Come in the house: go right in through the door.
  There are some people in there, have no fear.

LAURENCIA: Si los alcaldes entraran
  (que de uno soy hija yo),
  bien fuera entrar; mas si no . . .

COMENDADOR: Flores . . .

FLORES: Señor . . .

COMENDADOR: ¿Qué reparan
  en no hacer lo que les digo?

FLORES: Entrad, pues.

LAURENCIA: No nos agarre.

FLORES: Entrad; que sois necias.

PASCUALA: Arre;
  que echaréis luego el postigo.

FLORES: Entrad; que os quiere enseñar
  lo que trae de la guerra.

COMENDADOR (*aparte a Ortuño*):
  Si entraren, Ortuño, cierra.

  (*Entrase*)

LAURENCIA: Flores, dejadnos pasar.

ORTUÑO: ¿También venís presentadas
  con lo demás?

PASCUALA: ¡Bien a fe!
  Desvíese, no le dé . . .

FLORES: Basta; que son extremadas.

LAURENCIA: ¿No basta a vueso señor
  tanta carne presentada?

ORTUÑO: La vuestra es la que le agrada.

LAURENCIA: Reviente de mal dolor.

  (*Vanse*)

FLORES: ¡Muy buen recado llevamos!
  No se ha de poder sufrir
  lo que nos ha de decir
  cuando sin ellas nos vamos.

ORTUÑO: Quien sirve se obliga a esto.
  Si en algo desea medrar,
  o con paciencia ha de estar,
  o ha de despedirse presto.

  (*Vanse los dos*)

LAURENCIA: If our town burgesses went inside, too,
(I am the daughter of a councilman)
It would be perfectly all right; if not . . .

COMMANDER: Oh, Flores!

FLORES: Sire?

COMMANDER: You see how they refuse
To do what I have ordered?

FLORES (*To the girls*) Get inside!

LAURENCIA: Let go of us!

FLORES: Go in, you little fools!

PASCUALA: So you may lock the door on us? Not much!

FLORES: Go in; he wants to show you what he brought
You from the war.

COMMANDER (*Aside to Ortuño*): Ortuño, if perchance
The girls should come inside, you lock the door.
(*Commander Don Fernán enters the house.*)

LAURENCIA: Please let us go, good Flores.

ORTUÑO: Are you not
Included with the other gifts received?

PASCUALA: Not likely! Step aside, or else I'll scream.

FLORES: Enough, Ortuño; they are really mad.

LAURENCIA: Is not your master satisfied with all
The flesh received?

ORTUÑO: The kind he likes is yours.

LAURENCIA: I hope he bursts and dies a painful death!
(*Exeunt Laurencia and Pascuala*)

FLORES: A lovely bit of news we've got for him!
I hate to think of what he's going to say
When we go in the house without the girls.

ORTUÑO: All servants run that risk: to prosper, they
Must either bear it with a heart that's stout
Or else be ready quickly to get out!

(*Exeunt Flores and Ortuño*)

ESCENA 8

Habitación de los Reyes Católicos en Medina del Campo

Salen el Rey Don Fernando, la Reina Doña

Isabel, Manrique y acompañamiento

DOÑA ISABEL: Digo, señor, que conviene
el no haber descuido en esto,
por ver a Alfonso en tal puesto,
que su ejército previene.
Y es bien ganar por la mano
antes que el daño veamos;
que si no lo remediamos,
el ser muy cierto está llano.

REY: De Navarra y de Aragón
está el socorro seguro,
y de Castilla procuro
hacer la reformación,
de modo que el buen suceso
con la prevención se vea.

DOÑA ISABEL: Pues vuestra majestad crea
que el buen fin consiste en eso.

MANRIQUE: Aguardando tu licencia
dos regidores están
de Ciudad Real: ¿entrarán?

REY: No les nieguen mi presencia.

ESCENA 9

Salen dos regidores de Ciudad Real

REGIDOR 1º: Católico rey Fernando,
a quien ha enviado el cielo
desde Aragón a Castilla
para bien y amparo nuestro:

SCENE 8

The palace of the King and Queen in Medina del Campo

Enter King Ferdinand, Queen Isabella,

Don Manrique and retinue

ISABELLA: My lord, there must be no mistake in this.
We know Alfonso, King of Portugal,
Is ready and his army poised to march;
Hence we must strike before he hits us hard.
If we do not, we surely court defeat.

KING: Aid from Navarre and Aragon is sure,
And in Castile I shall regroup my force
In such a way that victory will crown
Our efforts.

ISABELLA: Rest assured, Your Majesty,
That full success depends upon such moves.

MANRIQUE: Two councilmen from Ciudad Real
Await your royal pleasure, sire. May they
Have audience?

KING: Let no one bar their way.

SCENE 9

Enter two councilmen

1ST COUNCILMAN: King Ferdinand, Most Catholic of Kings,
Whom Heaven sent to us from Aragon
To be the benefactor of Castile
As well as our protector: In the name

en nombre de Ciudad Real
a vuestro valor supremo
humildes nos presentamos,
el real amparo pidiendo.
A mucha dicha tuvimos
tener título de vuestros;
pero pudo derribarnos
deste honor el hado adverso.
El famoso don Rodrigo
Téllez Girón, cuyo esfuerzo
es en valor extremado,
aunque es en la edad tan tierno,
maestre de Calatrava,
el ensanche pretendiendo
y el honor de la encomienda,
nos puso apretado cerco.
Con valor nos prevenimos,
a su fuerza resistiendo,
tanto, que arroyos corrían
de la sangre de los muertos.
Tomó posesión, en fin;
pero no llegara a hacerlo,
a no le dar Fernán Gómez
orden, ayuda y consejo.
El queda en la posesión,
y sus vasallos seremos,
suyos, a nuestro pesar,
a no remediarlo presto.

REY: ¿Dónde queda Fernán Gómez?

REGIDOR 1º: En Fuenteovejuna creo,
por ser su villa, y tener
en ella casa y asiento.
Allí, con más libertad
de la que decir podemos,
tiene a los súbditos suyos
de todo contento ajenos.

REY: ¿Tenéis algún capitán?

Of Ciudad Real we now appear
Before you and most humbly beg a boon.
Protect us with your royal, valiant arms,
For we have been most happy in the past
To be your subjects; but an unkind fate
Has now deprived us of this honor, sire.
Rodrigo, Calatrava's Master, known
For courage and audacity despite
His tender years, besieged our city in
An effort to enlarge his own domains.
With valor we prepared to fight him off,
And battled so heroically that blood
In rivers ran from all our casualties.
At last he took possession of the town,
But this he never could have done without
The military aid and counsel of
Fernando Gómez. So the Master now
Remains in full possession of our town;
Your vassals will be his—much to our grief—
Unless your valiant sword brings prompt relief.

KING: Where is this Don Fernando Gómez now?

1ST COUNCILMAN: In Fuente Ovejuna, I believe,
For that is his domain and there he has
A home and an estate, Your Majesty.
It is beyond our power to describe
The way in which he grinds his vassals down
And keeps them in a state of discontent.

KING: But surely you must have some captain there?

REGIDOR 2º: Señor, el no haberle es cierto,
  pues no escapó ningún noble
  de preso, herido o de muerto.

DOÑA ISABEL: Ese caso no requiere
  ser de espacio remediado;
  que es dar al contrario osado
  el mismo valor que adquiere;
  y puede el de Portugal,
  hallando puerta segura
  entrar por Extremadura
  y causarnos mucho mal.

REY: Don Manrique, partid luego,
  llevando dos compañías;
  remediad sus demasías
  sin darles ningún sosiego.
  El conde de Cabra ir puede
  con vos; que es Córdoba osado,
  a quien nombre de soldado
  todo el mundo le concede;
  que éste es el medio mejor
  que la ocasión nos ofrece.

MANRIQUE: El acuerdo me parece
  como de tan gran valor.
  Pondré límite a su exceso,
  si el vivir en mí no cesa.

DOÑA ISABEL: Partiendo vos a la empresa,
  seguro está el buen suceso.

(Vanse todos)

ESCENA 10

Campo de   Fuenteovejuna

Salen Laurencia y Frondoso

LAURENCIA: A medio torcer los paños,
  quise, atrevido Frondoso,
  para no dar que decir,
  desviarme del arroyo;

2ND COUNCILMAN: Your Majesty, no nobleman is left;
  Without exception, not a one escaped.
  They all were captured, maimed, or put to death.
ISABELLA: Redress for this defeat brooks no delay:
  To do so is to give our enemy
  A chance to act with greater boldness still.
  The King of Portugal can strike us hard,
  For he can cross Extremadura's plain
  And safely enter through this gate to Spain.

KING: Good Don Manrique, take two companies
  And leave at once. Set right these grievous wrongs,
  And give no respite to the enemy.
  The Count of Cabra, one of Córdoba's
  Most brilliant soldiers, and esteemed by all
  As bold and brave, will ride along with you.
  Right now this is the best that we can do.

MANRIQUE: I think that your decision is most wise.
  This youth's ambitions I will bring to naught:
  As long as I draw breath, he shall be fought.

ISABELLA: With you, good Don Manrique, in command
  Our certain victory is near at hand.

                                    (*Exeunt omnes*)

SCENE 10

The countryside near Fuente Ovejuna

Enter Laurencia and Frondoso

LAURENCIA: I had to leave my washing but half done
  And quit the stream, Frondoso, all because
  Your bold advances have set this whole town

diciendo a tus demasías
que murmura el pueblo todo,
que me miras y te miro,
y todos nos traen sobre ojo.
Y como tú eres zagal,
de los que huellan, brioso,
y excediendo a los demás
vistes bizarro y costoso,
en todo el lugar no hay moza,
o mozo en el prado o soto,
que no se afirme diciendo
que ya para en uno somos;
y esperan todos el día
que el sacristán Juan Chamorro
nos eche de la tribuna,
en dejando los piporros[1].
Y mejor sus trojes veas
de rubio trigo en agosto
atestadas y colmadas,
y sus tinajas de mosto,
que tal imaginación
me ha llegado a dar enojo:
ni me desvela ni aflige,
ni en ella el cuidado pongo.

FRONDOSO: Tal me tienen tus desdenes,
bella Laurencia, que tomo,
en el peligro de verte,
la vida, cuando te oigo.
Si sabes que es mi intención
el desear ser tu esposo,
mal premio das a mi fe.

LAURENCIA: Es que yo no sé dar otro.

FRONDOSO: ¿Posible es que no te duelas
de verme tan cuidadoso
y que imaginando en ti
ni bebo, duermo ni como?

---

[1] *piporro*   instrumento músico de viento

To gossiping and saying you and I
Are flirting; everyone is watching us.
Because you strut around here more than most—
A dashing swain in flashy, costly clothes—
There is no village lass or country lad
Who does not say that we shall soon be one;
Now all of them await the festive day
When Sacristan Chamorro will suspend
The music and escort us from the church.
It would be better for these folk to watch
Their granaries fill up with golden grain
At harvest, or their earthen jars with wine.
Such gossip does annoy me, but I shall
Not worry or lose sleep because of it!

FRONDOSO: My beautiful Laurencia, when I gaze
Upon you and I hear you talk like that,
I am in such a state my very life
Is in grave danger due to your disdain.
You know it is my dearest wish to be
Your husband. Why do you repay me thus?

LAURENCIA: The fact is, I can be no other way.
FRONDOSO: How is it possible for you to feel
No grief when you observe my suffering?
Mere thinking of you robs me of my sleep;
I cannot eat my food, or even drink.

¿Posible es tanto rigor
en ese angélico rostro?
¡Viven los cielos que rabio!

LAURENCIA: Pues salúdate[1], Frondoso.

FRONDOSO: Ya te pido yo salud,
 y que ambos, como palomos,
 estemos, juntos los picos,
 con arrullos sonorosos,
 después de darnos la Iglesia . . .

LAURENCIA: Dilo a mi tío Juan Rojo;
 que aunque no te quiero bien,
 ya tengo algunos asomos.

FRONDOSO: ¡Ay de mí! El señor es éste.

LAURENCIA: Tirando viene a algún corzo.
 Escóndete en esas ramas.

FRONDOSO: Y ¡con qué celos me escondo!

        (*Ocúltase*)

ESCENA 11

Sale el Comendador con una ballesta

COMENDADOR: No es malo venir siguiendo
 un corcillo temeroso,
 y topar tan bella gama.

LAURENCIA: Aquí descansaba un poco
 de haber lavado unos paños;
 y así, al arroyo me torno,
 si manda su señoría.

COMENDADOR: Aquesos desdenes toscos
 afrentan, bella Laurencia,
 las gracias que el poderoso
 cielo te dió, de tal suerte,

[1] *salúdate* cúrate (con encantamentos)

But how can such unkindness harmonize
With that angelic face? I'm going mad!

LAURENCIA: Try taking medicine if you feel bad.
FRONDOSO: The medicine I need is your true love:
Let each of us, just like the turtledove,
With heart and soul begin to bill and coo
Together when the Church has joined us two.

LAURENCIA: Go ask my uncle; he's not fond of you,
But I might care a bit . . . in fact, I do!

FRONDOSO: Good heavens! Here comes Don Fernán, our lord.
LAURENCIA: He's hunting deer. Get in these bushes. Hide!

FRONDOSO: I go—but burn with jealousy inside.

(*Frondoso hides*)

SCENE 11

Enter the Commander, with a crossbow

COMMANDER: What luck to hunt a buck, and find a dear!

LAURENCIA: I was just resting here, my lord, because
I had been washing clothes down by the stream.
With your permission, I shall now return.

COMMANDER: That rude disdain insults the very charms
Almighty Heaven has bestowed on you,

que vienes a ser un monstruo.
Mas si otras veces pudiste
huir mi ruego amoroso,
ahora no quiere el campo,
amigo secreto y solo;
que tú sola no has de ser
tan soberbia, que tu rostro
huyas al señor que tienes,
teniéndome a mí en tan poco.
¿No se rindió Sebastiana,
mujer de Pedro Redondo,
con ser casadas entrambas,
y la de Martín del Pozo,
habiendo apenas pasado
dos días del desposorio?

LAURENCIA: Estas, señor, ya tenían,
de haber andado con otros,
el camino de agradaros;
porque también muchos mozos
merecieron sus favores.
Id con Dios, tras vueso corzo;
que a no veros con la cruz,
os tuviera por demonio,
pues tanto me perseguís.

COMENDADOR: ¡Qué estilo tan enfadoso!
Pongo la ballesta en tierra,
y a la práctica de manos
reduzgo melindres[1].

LAURENCIA: ¡Cómo!
¿Eso hacéis? ¿Estáis en vos?

COMENDADOR: No te defiendas.

(*Sale Frondoso y toma la ballesta*)

FRONDOSO (*Aparte*): Si tomo
la ballesta ¡vive el cielo
que no la ponga en el hombro!

---

[1] *melindres*   excesiva delicadeza

My fair Laurencia, and makes you a witch.
You may have fled my amorous advance
At other times, but now out here alone
These friendly fields will keep the secret well.
All by yourself you will not be so bold,
Nor spurn your master with such cold contempt.
Did not Sebastiana, Pedro's wife,
Give in to me, and Martin's wife as well,
And both those women only two days wed?

LAURENCIA: Those girls, my lord, already had affairs
Before they gave themselves to you: they had
Bestowed their favors on a lot of men.
Now go with God, and hunt your fleeing deer;
Indeed, if it were not for that red Cross
Upon your breast I'd think you were the Fiend,
The way that you have been pursuing me.

COMMANDER: How you offend me with that kind of talk!
Now I shall put my crossbow on the ground
And overcome your prudery by force.

LAURENCIA: What are you doing? Have you lost your mind?

COMMANDER: You must not struggle to defend yourself.
                    (*Frondoso comes out and picks up the bow*)
FRONDOSO (*Aside*): As I pick up this bow, I pray to God
I may not have to shoulder it and shoot!

COMENDADOR: Acaba, ríndete.

LAURENCIA: ¡Cielos,
    ayudadme ahora!

COMENDADOR: Solos
    estamos; no tengas miedo.

FRONDOSO: Comendador generoso,
    dejad la moza, o creed
    que de mi agravio y enojo
    será blanco vuestro pecho,
    aunque la cruz me da asombro.

COMENDADOR: ¡Perro, villano! . . .

FRONDOSO: No hay perro.
    Huye, Laurencia.

LAURENCIA: Frondoso,
    mira lo que haces.

FRONDOSO: Vete.

(*Vase*)

ESCENA 12

COMENDADOR: ¡Oh, mal haya el hombre loco,
    que se desciñe la espada!
    Que, de no espantar medroso
    la caza, me la quité.

FRONDOSO: Pues, pardiez, señor, si toco
    la nuez, que os he de apiolar.

COMENDADOR: Ya es ida. ¡Infame, alevoso,
    suelta la ballesta luego!
    ¡Suéltala, villano!

FRONDOSO: ¿Cómo?
    Que me quitaréis la vida.
    Y advertid que amor es sordo,
    y que no escucha palabras
    el día que está en su trono.

COMMANDER: Just stop that now! You might as well give in.
LAURENCIA: Good Lord above, come help me now I pray!

COMMANDER: We're all alone; you need not be afraid.

FRONDOSO: Most kind Commander, let the girl alone
  Or else your breast will be the target of
  My righteous wrath, despite the awe in which
  I hold that Cross you wear.

COMMANDER: You peasant dog!
FRONDOSO: I'm no dog, sire! Laurencia, run away!

LAURENCIA: Frondoso, have a care!

FRONDOSO: Now run, I say!

(Exit Laurencia)

SCENE 12

COMMANDER: Oh, what a fool to be without one's sword!
  I took it off lest I affright my prey.

FRONDOSO: By Heaven, sir! If I just loose this string
  I'll down you like a bird upon the wing!
COMMANDER: You lowborn, scurvy knave! She's run away!
  You peasant! Drop that bow at once, I say!

FRONDOSO: Why should I drop it? You would take my life.
  Be warned that love is deaf to reason and
  Does not heed words the day it takes command.

COMENDADOR: Pues ¿la espalda ha de volver
   un hombre tan valeroso
   a un villano? Tira, infame,
   tira, y guárdate; que rompo
   las leyes de caballero.

FRONDOSO: Eso, no. Yo me conformo
   con mi estado, y, pues me es
   guardar la vida forzoso,
   con la ballesta me voy.

                                                   (*Vase*)

COMENDADOR: ¡Peligro extraño y notorio!
   Mas yo tomaré venganza
   del agravio y del estorbo.
   ¡Que no cerrara con él!
   ¡Vive el cielo, que me corro! [1]

---

[1] *corro*   avergüenzo

COMMANDER: Should I, a wellborn man, just turn and flee
  Before a peasant? Shoot, you wretch! Shoot hard!
  I'll fight you though I am a knight! On guard!

FRONDOSO: I cannot shoot or fight you. As your serf
  I shall accept my station in this life.
  But since I'm forced to save my life today,
  I'll take this crossbow as I walk away.

  (*Exit Frondoso*)

COMMANDER: Who could foresee such danger—and how strange!
  If only I could get my hands on him.
  By God! I'll have revenge for this attack!
  I shall not rest until I've paid him back!

ACTO SEGUNDO

ESCENA 1

Plaza de Fuenteovejuna

Salen Esteban y un regidor

ESTEBAN: Así tenga salud, como parece,
que no se saque más ahora el pósito.
El año apunta mal, y el tiempo crece,
y es mejor que el sustento esté en depósito,
aunque lo contradicen más de trece.

REGIDOR: Yo siempre he sido, al fin, deste propósito,
en gobernar en paz esta república.

ESTEBAN: Hagamos dello a Fernán Gómez súplica.
No se puede sufrir que estos astrólogos,
en las cosas futuras ignorantes,
nos quieran persuadir con largos prólogos
los secretos a Dios sólo importantes.
¡Bueno es que, presumiendo de teólogos,
hagan un tiempo el de después y antes!
Y pidiendo el presente lo importante,
al más sabio veréis más ignorante.
¿Tienen ellos las nubes en su casa
y el proceder de las celestes lumbres?
¿Por dónde ven lo que en el cielo pasa,
para darnos con ello pesadumbres?

60

ACT TWO

❦

SCENE 1

The village square in Fuente Ovejuna

Enter Esteban and a Councilman

ESTEBAN: In my opinion, no more grain should be
  Removed from our town granary right now.
  The year is wearing on, the crops look poor,
  And it is best to let the grain remain
  In storage bins, despite what many say.

COUNCILMAN: My own idea of ruling the town well
  Has always been, indeed, exactly that.

ESTEBAN: Then let us make a plea to Don Fernán
  About this matter. We cannot stand by
  And let astrologers who do not know
  The future sway us with their long harangues
  Concerning secrets known to God alone.
  The way they put on high and mighty airs,
  As if they were great theologians,
  And mix what is to come with what has passed!
  The present is what's vital to us now,
  But there you'll find the wisest is most dense:
  You'd think they had the rain clouds in their homes,
  And could control the great celestial orbs!
  How can they tell what's happening on high,
  And frighten us with all their fol-de-rol?

Ellos en el sembrar nos ponen tasa:
daca el trigo, cebada y las legumbres,
calabazas, pepinos y mostazas . . .
Ellos son, a la fe, las calabazas.
Luego cuentan que muere una cabeza,
y después viene a ser en Trasilvania;
que el vino será poco; y la cerveza
sobrará por las partes de Alemania;
que se helará en Gascuña la cereza,
y que habrá muchos tigres en Hircania.
Y al cabo, que se siembre o no se siembre,
el año se remata por diciembre.

ESCENA 2

Salen el licenciado Leonelo y Barrildo

LEONELO: A fe que no ganéis la palmatoria,
porque ya está ocupado el mentidero.
BARRILDO: ¿Cómo os fué en Salamanca?

LEONELO: Es larga historia.
BARRILDO: Un Bártulo seréis.

LEONELO: Ni aun un barbero.
Es como digo, cosa muy notoria
en esta facultad lo que os refiero.
BARRILDO: Sin duda que venís buen estudiante.
LEONELO: Saber he procurado lo importante.
BARRILDO: Después que vemos tanto libro impreso,
no hay nadie que de sabio no presuma.
LEONELO: Antes que ignoran más siento por eso,
por no se reducir a breve suma;
porque la confusión, con el exceso,
los intentos resuelve en vana espuma;
y aquel que de leer tiene más uso,
de ver letreros sólo está confuso.
No niego yo que de imprimir el arte
mil ingenios sacó de entre la jerga,

They set the time for us to sow the seed:
For wheat and barley, and for peas and beans,
Cucumbers, mustard plants, and pumpkins, too.
It's they who are the pumpkin heads, I swear!
And then they tell us that a cow will die,
And it occurs—in Transylvania!
They say that wine will be in short supply,
That parts of Germany will have much beer;
The cherry crop in France will surely freeze
And tigers will abound in Persia's plains.
But whether we decide to sow or not,
The year to its conclusion always wends,
And on December thirty-first it ends!

SCENE 2

Enter Leonelo and Barrildo

LEONELO: Upon my faith! We did not get here first:
  I see the square's already occupied.

BARRILDO: Now tell me how you liked your student life
  At Salamanca University?

LEONELO: It's quite a story.

BARRILDO: You must be by now
  A learnèd doctor.

LEONELO: I am not as yet
  A simple barber! I've been telling you
  About the escapades at college there.

BARRILDO: But doubtless you have learned your lessons well.

LEONELO: I've tried to learn what's most important, yes.

BARRILDO: So many books are being printed now,
  There's not a soul but boasts he is a sage!

LEONELO: It seems to me they know less than before,
  Because the great excess of books creates
  Confusion in the minds of readers now,
  And avid readers are the most confused
  By all the titles. I do not deny
  The art of printing has saved many men
  Of genius from oblivion, and has

y que parece que en sagrada parte
sus obras guarda y contra el tiempo alberga,
y éste las distribuye y las reparte.
Débese esta invención a Gutemberga,
un famoso tudesco de Maguncia,
en quien la fama su valor renuncia.
Mas muchos que opinión tuvieron grave
por imprimir sus obras la perdieron;
tras esto, con el nombre del que sabe,
muchos sus ignorancias imprimieron.
Otros, en quien la baja envidia cabe,
sus locos desatinos escribieron,
y con nombre de aquel que aborrecían,
impresos por el mundo los envían.

BARRILDO: No soy desa opinión.

LEONELO: El ignorante
es justo que se vengue del letrado.

BARRILDO: Leonelo, la impresión es importante.

LEONELO: Sin ella muchos siglos se han pasado,
y no vemos que en éste se levante
un Jerónimo santo, un Agustino.

BARRILDO: Dejadlo y asentaos, que estáis mohino.

ESCENA 3

Salen Juan Rojo y otro labrador

JUAN ROJO: No hay en cuatro haciendas para un dote,
si es que las vistas han de ser al uso;
que el hombre que es curioso es bien que note
que en esto el barrio y vulgo anda confuso.

LABRADOR: ¿Qué hay del Comendador? No os alborote.

JUAN ROJO: ¡Cuál a Laurencia en ese campo puso!

LABRADOR: ¿Quién fué cual él tan bárbaro y lascivo?
¡Colgado le vea yo de aquel olivo!

Conserved their works like holy writ and kept
Them from the ravages of time until
Released and passed on to posterity.
A famous German, Gutenberg of Mainz,
Whose fame will long endure, invented it.
But many who were once considered wise
Have lost their reputation since their works
Appeared in print; moreover, there are some
Who put their ignorance in print and pass
It off as wisdom. Others, envious
Of rivals, sign the names of those they hate
To trash, then spread it through the world in print.

BARRILDO: I do not share those views.

LEONELO: The stupid man
Thus takes his vengeance on the learnèd one.

BARRILDO: But printing is important, all the same.

LEONELO: The world got on without it very well
For many centuries, and in this one
There is no St. Jerome or Augustine!

BARRILDO: There is no need to work up so much heat;
Let's leave the topic now and find a seat.

SCENE 3

Enter Juan Rojo and a farmer

ROJO: Yes, four whole farms are not enough to make
A dowry by the standards of today:
To understand this, look at how the town
And people—all confused—have gone astray!

FARMER: Please do not get upset. What do you hear
About Commander Don Fernán?

ROJO: He tried
To seize Laurencia in these fields today.

FARMER: The lewd, licentious beast! I'd love to see
Him hanging high from yonder olive tree!

ESCENA 4

Salen el Comendador, Ortuño y Flores

COMENDADOR: Dios guarde la buena gente.

REGIDOR: ¡Oh, señor!

COMENDADOR: Por vía mía,
que se estén.

ESTEBAN: Vusiñoría
adonde suele se siente,
que en pie estaremos muy bien.

COMENDADOR: Digo que se han de sentar.

ESTEBAN: De los buenos es honrar,
que no es posible que den
honra los que no la tienen.

COMENDADOR: Siéntense; hablaremos algo.

ESTEBAN: ¿Vió vusiñoría el galgo?

COMENDADOR: Alcalde, espantados vienen
esos criados de ver
tan notable ligereza.

ESTEBAN: Es una extremada pieza.
Pardiez, que puede correr
al lado de un delincuente
o de un cobarde en quistión[1].

COMENDADOR: Quisiera en esta ocasión
que le echarais diligente
a una liebre que por pies
por momentos se me va.

ESTEBAN: Sí haré, por Dios. ¿Dónde está?

COMENDADOR: Allá; vuestra hija es.

ESTEBAN: ¡Mi hija!

COMENDADOR: Sí.

---

[1] *quistión*   persecución

SCENE 4

Enter Flores, Ortuño and the Commander

COMMANDER: A good day to you all, my people!

COUNCILMAN (*Rising*):   Sire!

COMMANDER: Please do not rise: stay seated, everyone.

ESTEBAN: Your Lordship, kindly take the seat reserved
   For you; we are content to stand like this.

COMMANDER: I said you should sit down.

ESTEBAN: All decent folk
   Are glad to honor rank: it is but right,
   For only those with honor in themselves
   Can render it.

COMMANDER: Sit down; let's talk a while.

ESTEBAN: And did Your Lordship see the hound we sent?

COMMANDER: My servants are astonished at its speed.

ESTEBAN: It is, I swear, a rare and noble beast,
   Which can track down and overtake
   A skulking convict who is being sought.

COMMANDER: I would prefer in this case that you send
   It out to hunt a certain piece of game
   That keeps eluding me.

ESTEBAN: Of course I shall!
   By Heaven, tell me what and where it is!

COMMANDER: I mean your daughter.

ESTEBAN: What! My daughter, sire?

COMMANDER: Indeed.

ESTEBAN: Pues ¿es buena
para alcanzada de vos?

COMENDADOR: Reñidla, alcalde, por Dios.

ESTEBAN: ¿Cómo?

COMENDADOR: Ha dado en darme pena.
Mujer hay, y principal,
de alguno que está en la plaza,
que dió, a la primera traza,
traza de verme.

ESTEBAN: Hizo mal;
y vos, señor, no andáis bien
en hablar tan libremente.

COMENDADOR: ¡Oh, qué villano elocuente!
¡Ah, Flores! haz que le den
la *Política,* en que lea
de Aristóteles.

ESTEBAN: Señor,
debajo de vuestro honor
vivir el pueblo desea.
Mirad que en Fuenteovejuna
hay gente muy principal.

LEONELO: ¿Vióse desvergüenza igual?

COMENDADOR: Pues ¿he dicho cosa alguna
de que os pese, regidor?

REGIDOR: Lo que decís es injusto;
no lo digáis, que no es justo
que nos quitéis el honor.

COMENDADOR: ¿Vosotros honor tenéis?
¡Qué freiles de Calatrava!

REGIDOR: Alguno acaso se alaba
de la cruz que le ponéis,
que no es de sangre tan limpia.

COMENDADOR: Y ¿ensúciola yo juntando
la mía a la vuestra?

REGIDOR: Cuando
es mal, más tiñe que alimpia.

COMENDADOR: De cualquier suerte que sea,
vuestras mujeres se honran.

ESTEBAN: Is she fair game for you, my lord?

COMMANDER: I wish that you would urge her, Mr. Mayor.

ESTEBAN: You mean . . .

COMMANDER: She is determined to resist.
 But I could name a woman of high class,
 The wife of one now present in this square,
 Who yielded to me at my first advance.

ESTEBAN: Then she did wrong, my lord, and you do wrong
 Yourself in speaking freely of it thus.

COMMANDER: My, my! A peasant who is eloquent!
 Oh, Flores! See that he receives a gift
 Of Aristotle's *Politics* to read.

ESTEBAN: My lord, this village fain would live in peace
 Beneath your rule. Consider that there are
 In Fuente Ovejuna men of worth.

LEONELO: What shameless things our Don Fernán has said!

COMMANDER: Have I said anything that bothers you,
 Good councilman?

COUNCILMAN: Your words are most unjust.
 You should not say such things: it is not right
 That you besmirch our honor in this way.

COMMANDER: Do you have honor? Next you'll claim to be
 Bold Knights of Calatrava, I suppose!

COUNCILMAN: Perhaps there are some men who boast about
 That Cross you wear, and are of impure blood.

COMMANDER: Do I pollute your blood when I mix mine
 With peasant stock?

COUNCILMAN: When evil lust is there,
 It fouls our blood more than it purifies.

COMMANDER: Your womenfolk are honored, all the same.

ESTEBAN: Esas palabras deshonran;
las obras no hay quien las crea.

COMENDADOR: ¡Qué cansado villanaje!
¡Ah! Bien hayan las ciudades,
que a hombres de calidades
no hay quien sus gustos ataje;
allá se precian casados
que visiten sus mujeres.

ESTEBAN: No harán; que con esto quieres
que vivamos descuidados.
En las ciudades hay Dios
y más presto quien castiga.

COMENDADOR: Levantaos de aquí.

ESTEBAN: ¿Que diga
lo que escucháis por los dos?

COMENDADOR: Salí[1] de la plaza luego;
no quede ninguno aquí.

ESTEBAN: Ya nos vamos.

COMENDADOR: Pues no ansí.[2]

FLORES: Que te reportes te ruego.

COMENDADOR: Querrían hacer corrillo
los villanos en mi ausencia.

ORTUÑO: Ten un poco de paciencia.

COMENDADOR: De tanta me maravillo.
Cada uno de por sí
se vayan hasta sus casas.

LEONELO: ¡Cielo! ¿Que por esto pasas?

ESTEBAN: Ya yo me voy por aquí.

(*Vanse los labradores*)

---

[1] *Salí*   salid

[2] *ansí*   así

ESTEBAN: Those words dishonor you: we simply can't
　　Believe you mean—or do—the things you say.

COMMANDER: How dull you peasants are! Give me the life
　　In cities, where we men of quality
　　Are able to enjoy our pleasures free
　　From interference; there, the men are proud
　　To know their wives attract our roving eye.

ESTEBAN: That can't be true. What you would really like
　　Is greater laxness in our way of life.
　　In cities, too, there is God's justice and,
　　Much closer still, the swift revenge of man.

COMMANDER: Get out of here!

ESTEBAN: 　　　　　　　　　Does that mean me alone?

COMMANDER: I order you to leave this square at once,
　　The lot of you! Let not one soul remain!

ESTEBAN: We'll leave right now.

COMMANDER: 　　　　　　　But not in groups like that!

FLORES: Control yourself, my lord, I beg of you.

COMMANDER: While I was gone those peasants must have formed
　　In bands to plot against me.

ORTUÑO: 　　　　　　　　　Patience, sire.

COMMANDER: The wonder is I've shown so much of it.
　　Now go on home—but each one by himself!

LEONELO: Good heavens! You endure this every day?

ESTEBAN: I'm leaving now; I think I'll go this way.

　　　　　　　　　　　　　　(*The townsfolk leave*)

ESCENA 5

Comendador, Ortuño y Flores

COMENDADOR: ¿Qué os parece desta gente?

ORTUÑO: No saben disimular,
y no quieren escuchar
el disgusto que se siente.

COMENDADOR: Estos ¿se igualan conmigo?

FLORES: Que no es aqueso igualarse.

COMENDADOR: Y el villano ¿ha de quedarse
con ballesta y sin castigo?

FLORES: Anoche pensé que estaba
a la puerta de Laurencia,
y a otro, que su presencia
y su capilla imitaba,
de oreja a oreja le di
un beneficio famoso.

COMENDADOR: ¿Dónde estará aquel Frondoso?

FLORES: Dicen que anda por ahí.

COMENDADOR: ¡Por ahí se atreve a andar
hombre que matarme quiso!

FLORES: Como el ave sin aviso,
o como el pez, viene a dar
al reclamo o al anzuelo.

COMENDADOR: ¡Que a un capitán cuya espada
tiemblan Córdoba y Granada,
un labrador, un mozuelo
ponga una ballesta al pecho!
El mundo se acaba, Flores.

FLORES: Como eso pueden amores.

ORTUÑO: Y pues que vives, sospecho
que grande amistad le debes.

SCENE 5

The Commander, Ortuño and Flores

COMMANDER: What think you of these peasants here?

ORTUÑO: My lord,
They are but simple folk who cannot hide
Their feelings: hence they do not wish to hear
About unpleasant things.

COMMANDER: But do they rank
Themselves as equal to me?

FLORES: It is not
Exactly that they think they're equal, sire . . .

COMMANDER: And what about that peasant who walked off
With my best crossbow? Shall he go scot-free?

FLORES: Last night I thought I saw him at the door
Outside Laurencia's house, and slashed his throat
From ear to ear—but it was someone else
Who looked like him.

COMMANDER: Where can that scurvy knave
Frondoso be?

FLORES: Around somewhere, they say.

COMMANDER: A man who tried to kill me dares to show
Himself around these parts?

FLORES: He is just like
An unsuspecting bird who will be snared,
Or else a fish who will be hooked one day.

COMMANDER: To think a peasant—just a youth—should point
A crossbow at the breast of one whose sword
Makes Córdoba and all Granada quake!
I swear, this world is coming to an end!

FLORES: Love nerves men on to do a thing like that.

ORTUÑO: Since you are still alive, my lord, I do
Believe that you must be a friend of his!

COMENDADOR: Yo he disimulado, Ortuño;
que si no, de punta a puño,
antes de dos horas breves,
pasara todo el lugar;
que hasta que llegue ocasión
al freno de la razón
hago la venganza estar.
¿Qué hay de Pascuala?

FLORES: Responde
que anda ahora por casarse.

COMENDADOR: ¿Hasta allá quiere fiarse? . . .

FLORES: En fin, te remite donde
te pagarán de contado.

COMENDADOR: ¿Qué hay de Olalla?

ORTUÑO: Una graciosa
respuesta.

COMENDADOR: Es moza briosa.
¿Cómo?

ORTUÑO: Que su desposado
anda tras ella estos días
celoso de mis recados
y de que con tus criados
a visitarla venías;
pero que si se descuida
entrarás como primero.

COMENDADOR: ¡Bueno, a fe de caballero!
Pero el villanejo cuida . . .

ORTUÑO: Cuida, y anda por los aires.

COMENDADOR: ¿Qué hay de Inés?

FLORES: ¿Cuál?

COMENDADOR: La de Antón.

FLORES: Para cualquier ocasión
te ha ofrecido sus donaires.
Habléla por el corral,
por donde has de entrar si quieres.

COMENDADOR: A las fáciles mujeres
quiero bien y pago mal.
Si éstas supiesen, ¡oh, Flores!
estimarse en lo que valen.

COMMANDER: Ortuño, I have feigned this friendship, else
  In two short hours I'd have put this town
  All to the sword—just run them through and through.
  But I am letting reason hold revenge
  In check until the proper time arrives.
  About Pascuala, now: what news of her?

FLORES: She tells me she is getting married soon.

COMMANDER: She'd go as far as that . . . ?
FLORES: In short, my lord,
  She's fixing things so you'll be paid back—fast!
COMMANDER: Olalla—what of her?
ORTUÑO: A smart reply.

COMMANDER: Now there's a lively wench! What did she say?

ORTUÑO: Her husband's watching her these days because
  He is suspicious of the notes I bring,
  And of your visits with your servants, sire.
  But once he's off his guard, you may return.

COMMANDER: Good news, upon my solemn word! But that
  Shrewd peasant is a very watchful one . . .
ORTUÑO: He is, my lord, and quick to anger, too.
COMMANDER: And what about Inés?
FLORES: Inés? Which one?
COMMANDER: The wife of Anton.
FLORES: She has offered you
  Her charms whenever you are ready, sire.
  I spoke to her in the corral: you may
  Go in that way at any time you wish.
COMMANDER: These easy women! How I like them—but
  I pay them poorly. If they knew their worth
  They'd set a higher price upon themselves.

FLORES: No hay disgustos que se igualen
    a contrastar sus favores.
    Rendirse presto desdice
    de la esperanza del bien;
    mas hay mujeres también
    porque el filósofo dice
    que apetecen a los hombres
    como la forma desea
    la materia; y que esto sea
    así, no hay de qué te asombres.

COMENDADOR: Un hombre de amores loco
    huélgase que a su accidente
    se le rindan fácilmente,
    mas después las tiene en poco,
    y el camino de olvidar,
    al hombre más obligado
    es haber poco costado
    lo que pudo desear.

ESCENA 6

Sale Cimbranos.

CIMBRANOS: ¿Está aquí el Comendador?

ORTUÑO: ¿No le ves en tu presencia?

CIMBRANOS: ¡Oh gallardo Fernán Gómez!
    Trueca la verde montera
    en el blanco morrïón
    y el gabán en armas nuevas;
    que el maestre de Santiago
    y el conde de Cabra cercan
    a don Rodrigo Girón,
    por la castellana reina,
    en Ciudad Real; de suerte
    que no es mucho que se pierda
    lo que en Calatrava sabes
    que tanta sangre le cuesta.
    Ya divisan con las luces,
    desde las altas almenas,

FLORES: But easy conquest takes away the joy
  Of victory: anticipation's glow
  Is dimmed if they surrender rapidly.
  There are some women who desire men
  As abstract form needs substance, we are told
  By wise philosophers. If this be so,
  There is no cause for you to be surprised.

COMMANDER: But when a man is crazed by one desire,
  He's glad they yield themselves to him so fast,
  Though afterward he'll scorn them, and forget;
  For even the most grateful will have lost
  Respect for women won at no great cost.

SCENE 6

Enter Cimbranos

CIMBRANOS: Is Don Fernán, the Grand Commander, here?
ORTUÑO: But don't you see him there before you now?
CIMBRANOS: Oh, valiant Don Fernán! The time has come
  To doff your hunter's cap of green and don
  Your shining helmet; to take off that cloak
  You're wearing and put on your coat of mail.
  Queen Isabella of Castile has sent
  The Master of Santiago and the Count
  Of Cabra to retake Ciudad Real,
  Where Don Rodrigo is surrounded now.
  You know how much of Calatrava's blood
  Was spilled to win that town, and now we stand
  To lose it. From our lofty battlements
  We see their banners by their campfires' light:

los castillos y leones
y barras aragonesas.
Y aunque el rey de Portugal
honrar a Girón quisiera,
no hará poco en que el maestre
a Almagro con vida vuelva.
Ponte a caballo, señor;
que sólo con que te vean
se volverán a Castilla.

COMENDADOR: No prosigas; tente, espera.
Haz, Ortuño, que en la plaza
toquen luego una trompeta.
¿Qué soldados tengo aquí?

ORTUÑO: Pienso que tienes cincuenta.

COMENDADOR: Pónganse a caballo todos.

CIMBRANOS: Si no caminas apriesa,
Ciudad Real es del rey.

COMENDADOR: No hayas miedo que lo sea.

(Vanse)

ESCENA 7

Campo de Fuenteovejuna

*Salen Mengo, Laurencia y Pascuala,
huyendo*

PASCUALA: No te apartes de nosotras.

MENGO: Pues ¿a qué tenéis temor?

LAURENCIA: Mengo, a la villa es mejor
que vamos[1] unas con otras
(pues que no hay hombre ninguno),
por que no demos con él.

MENGO: ¡Que este demonio crüel
nos sea tan importuno!

[1] *vamos*   vayamos

The lions and the castles of Castile,
And Aragon's bright bars. Although the King
Of Portugal would like to honor his
Firm pledge of aid to Don Rodrigo, our
Young Master will be lucky to escape
Alive and get back to Almagro, sire.
Mount up! The very sight of you, we feel,
Should send them flying back into Castile!

COMMANDER: You've said enough; do not go on; attend.
Ortuño, have them sound a trumpet blast
At once, here in the square. How many men
Have I on call here?

ORTUÑO: Fifty, I believe.

COMMANDER: Bid all to horse at once!

CIMBRANOS: And ride full speed:
The fall of Ciudad Real is near.

COMMANDER: The King shall not regain it, never fear.

(*Exeunt omnes*)

SCENE 7

The countryside near Fuente Ovejuna

Enter Mengo, then Laurencia and Pascuala, fleeing

PASCUALA: Don't leave us!

MENGO: Even here you are afraid?

LAURENCIA: 'Tis best that we girls travel into town
Together, Mengo, when there is no man
With us, lest we meet Don Fernán alone.

MENGO: That vile, relentless devil plagues us all!

LAURENCIA: No nos deja a sol ni a sombra.

MENGO: ¡Oh! Rayo del cielo baje
que sus locuras ataje.

LAURENCIA: Sangrienta fiera le nombra;
arsénico y pestilencia
del lugar.

MENGO: Hanme contado
que Frondoso, aquí en el prado,
para librarte, Laurencia,
le puso a pecho una jara.

LAURENCIA: Los hombres aborrecía,
Mengo; mas desde aquel día
los miro con otra cara.
¡Gran valor tuvo Frondoso!
Pienso que le ha de costar
la vida.

MENGO: Que del lugar
se vaya, será forzoso.

LAURENCIA: Aunque ya le quiero bien,
eso mismo le aconsejo;
mas recibe mi consejo
con ira, rabia y desdén;
y jura el Comendador
que le ha de colgar de un pie.

PASCUALA: ¡Mal garrotillo le dé!

MENGO: Mala pedrada es mejor.
¡Voto al sol, si le tirara
con la que llevo al apero,
que al sonar el crujidero
al casco se la encajara!
No fué Sábalo, el romano,
tan vicioso por jamás.

LAURENCIA: Heliogábalo dirás,
más que una fiera inhumano.

MENGO: Pelicálvaro, o quien fué,
que yo no entiendo de historia;

LAURENCIA: We have no respite, night or day, from him.

MENGO: May Heaven send a thunderbolt to put
An end to him and all his mad designs!

LAURENCIA: I'd call him more a beast that thirsts for blood,
A plague and poison that infects the realm.

MENGO: They tell me that right here in these green fields
Frondoso aimed a crossbow at his heart
To set you free, Laurencia.

LAURENCIA: I had looked
Upon all men with loathing up until
That day, but now regard them, Mengo, in
Another light. How brave Frondoso was!
I fear his action may cost him his life.

MENGO: He will, of course, be forced to leave this town.

LAURENCIA: Although I've come to love him well, I keep
On urging him to do that very thing,
But he disdains my pleas with scornful wrath.
That foul Commander swears that he will string
Frondoso up and hang him by the heels.

PASCUALA: May he himself be garroted to death!

MENGO: I'd rather see him stoned to death. I swear
By yonder sun that if I used the sling
I carry when I'm herding sheep, I'd hurl
A rock so hard that it would crack his skull!
Old Roman Sábulus was never quite
So vicious.

LAURENCIA: Heliogábulus, you mean:
The one who was more brutish than a beast.

MENGO: Well, hellish Gábulus, whatever he
Was named; I never understood too much
Of history. But his foul memory

mas su cativa[1] memoria
vencida de éste se ve.
¿Hay hombre en naturaleza
como Fernán Gómez?

PASCUALA: No;
que parece que le dió
de una tigre la aspereza.

ESCENA 8

Sale Jacinta

JACINTA: ¡Dadme socorro, por Dios,
si la amistad os obliga!

LAURENCIA: ¿Qué es esto, Jacinta amiga?

PASCUALA: Tuyas lo somos las dos.

JACINTA: Del Comendador criados,
que van a Ciudad Real,
más de infamia natural
que de noble acero armados,
me quieren llevar a él.

LAURENCIA: Pues Jacinta, Dios te libre;
que cuando contigo es libre,
conmigo será crüel.

(Vase)

PASCUALA: Jacinta, yo no soy hombre
que te pueda defender.

(Vase)

MENGO: Yo sí lo tengo de ser,
porque tengo el ser y el nombre.
Llégate, Jacinta, a mí.

JACINTA: ¿Tienes armas?

MENGO: Las primeras
del mundo.

JACINTA: ¡Oh, si las tuvieras!

MENGO: Piedras hay, Jacinta, aquí.

---

[1] *cativa*   cautiva (infortunada)

Is far surpassed by this beast Don Fernán.
Has Nature ever fashioned man so vile?

PASCUALA: She has not; no, indeed; it seems that she
Gave him a tiger's fell ferocity.

SCENE 8

Enter Jacinta

JACINTA: Oh, help me, for the love of God, if you
Hold any friendship in your heart for me!

LAURENCIA: What is it, friend Jacinta?

PASCUALA: We are both
Your friends.

JACINTA: En route to Ciudad Real,
Some henchmen of Commander Don Fernán
(Armed more in infamy than martial steel)
Intend to drag me off with them to him.

LAURENCIA: May God protect you, then, Jacinta dear:
If Don Fernán is bold with you, with me
He would be cruelty itself.

(*Exit Laurencia.*)

PASCUALA: I'm not
A man: I cannot fight in your defense.

(*Exit Pascuala.*)

MENGO: Then I'm elected, for I have the name
And gender of a man. Jacinta, come
Here close to me.

JACINTA: But have you any arms?

MENGO: The first and best in all the world.

JACINTA: Would that
You had some weapons!

MENGO: There are stones about.

ESCENA 9

Salen Flores y Ortuño; Soldados

FLORES: ¿Por los pies pensabas irte?

JACINTA: ¡Mengo, muerta soy!

MENGO: Señores . . .
  ¡A estos pobres labradores! . . .

ORTUÑO: Pues ¿tú quieres persuadirte
  a defender la mujer?

MENGO: Con los ruegos la defiendo;
  que soy su deudo y pretendo
  guardarla, si puede ser.

FLORES: Quitadle luego la vida.

MENGO: ¡Voto al sol, si me emberrincho,[1]
  y el cáñamo me descincho,
  que la llevéis bien vendida!

ESCENA 10

Salen el Comendador y Cimbranos

COMENDADOR: ¿Qué es eso? ¡A cosas tan viles
  me habéis de hacer apear!

FLORES: Gente deste vil lugar
  (que ya es razón que aniquiles,
  pues en nada te da gusto)
  a nuestras armas se atreve.

MENGO: Señor, si piedad os mueve
  de suceso tan injusto,
  castigad estos soldados,
  que con vuestro nombre ahora
  roban una labradora
  a esposo y padres honrados;
  y dadme licencia a mí.
  que se la pueda llevar.

  [1] *emberrincho*   emberrenchino

SCENE 9

Enter Flores and Ortuño, with soldiers

FLORES: You thought that you could run away from us?

JACINTA: I'm ruined, Mengo!

MENGO: Surely, gentlemen,
  You don't molest poor country folk like this?

ORTUÑO: So you've decided to defend the wench?

MENGO: I shall defend her with my pleas, for she
  And I are kin, and I shall do my best
  To save her if I can.

FLORES: Let's kill him, quick!

MENGO: I swear by yonder sun! If I fly off
  Into a rage and loose my sling from here,
  You may take her, but it will cost you dear!

SCENE 10

Enter the Commander, accompanied by Cimbranos

COMMANDER: What is all this? Must I dismount because
  Of petty quarrels?

FLORES: Sire, the commoners
  Of this vile town are challenging our arms,
  And you should raze it to the ground. To you
  It is a source of nothing but distress.

MENGO: My lord, if pity move your heart to see
  An unjust deed, then punish these two men
  Who in your name are dragging this poor girl
  Away from honest parents and her spouse,
  And give me leave to take her to her house.

COMENDADOR: Licencia les quiero dar . . .
para vengarse de ti.
Suelta la honda.

MENGO: ¡Señor! . . .

COMENDADOR: Flores, Ortuño, Cimbranos,
con ella le atad las manos.

MENGO: ¿Así volvéis por su honor?

COMENDADOR: ¿Qué piensan Fuenteovejuna
y sus villanos de mí?

MENGO: Señor, ¿en qué os ofendí,
ni el pueblo en cosa ninguna?

FLORES: ¿Ha de morir?

COMENDADOR: No ensuciéis
las armas, que habéis de honrar
en otro mejor lugar.

ORTUÑO: ¿Qué mandas?

COMENDADOR: Que lo azotéis.
Llevadle, y en ese roble
le atad y le desnudad,
y con las riendas . . .

MENGO: ¡Piedad!
¡Piedad, pues sois hombre noble!

COMENDADOR: Azotadle hasta que salten
los hierros de las correas.

MENGO: ¡Cielos! ¿A hazañas tan feas
queréis que castigos falten?

(*Flores, Ortuño y Cimbranos se llevan a Mengo*)

ESCENA 11

Comendador, Jacinta y Soldados

COMENDADOR: Tú, villana, ¿por qué huyes?
¿Es mejor un labrador
que un hombre de mi valor?

COMMANDER: I'll give my leave—for them to punish you!
Now drop that hempen sling you hold.

MENGO: But sire . . .

COMMANDER: Ortuño, Flores, and Cimbranos, tie
His hands with it.

MENGO: And think you thus to save
Her honor?

COMMANDER: What do all you peasants think
Of me in Fuente Ovejuna, eh?

MENGO: But sire, have I offended you at all,
Or have the townsfolk?

FLORES: Shall we run him through?

COMMANDER: Don't soil your weapons, which you soon will use
More honorably on another field.

ORTUÑO: What are your orders?

COMMANDER: Flog him! Strip him first,
Then tie him to that oak, and with your reins . . .

MENGO: Have pity, sire; have pity, as you are
A nobleman!

COMMANDER: . . . just lash and lash until
The buckles loosen from the leather straps!

MENGO: Dear Heaven, canst thou fail to hear my pleas?
Thy punishment on such vile deeds as these!

(*Mengo is dragged off by Flores, Ortuño and Cimbranos*)

SCENE 11

Soldiers continue standing in the background

COMMANDER: And you, girl: tell me why you ran away.
Is some crude peasant better than a man
Of worth like me?

JACINTA: ¡Harto bien me restituyes
el honor que me han quitado
en llevarme para ti!

COMENDADOR: ¿En quererte llevar?

JACINTA: Sí;
porque tengo un padre honrado,
que si en alto nacimiento
no te iguala, en las costumbres
te vence.

COMENDADOR: Las pesadumbres
y el villano atrevimiento
no templan bien un airado.
Tira[1] por ahi.

JACINTA: ¿Con quién?

COMENDADOR: Conmigo.

JACINTA: Míralo bien.

COMENDADOR: Para tu mal lo he mirado.
Ya no mía, del bagaje
del ejército has de ser.

JACINTA: No tiene el mundo poder
para hacerme, viva, ultraje.

COMENDADOR: Ea, villana, camina.

JACINTA: ¡Piedad, señor!

COMENDADOR: No hay piedad.

JACINTA: ¡Apelo de tu crueldad
a la justicia divina!

(Llévanla y vanse)

ESCENA 12

Calle en Fuente Ovejuna

Salen Laurencia y Frondoso

LAURENCIA: ¿Cómo así a venir te atreves,
sin temer tu daño?

[1] *Tira* Vete

JACINTA: A fine way you restore
  The honor I have lost by being brought
  To you!

COMMANDER: It's lost because I ordered them
  To bring you here?

JACINTA: It is, indeed! I have
  An honored father who, although he is
  Not high-born as you are, surpasses you
  In virtuous behavior.

COMMANDER: Bold remarks
  And peasant insolence will hardly serve
  To cool an angry man. Now come along!

JACINTA: With whom?

COMMANDER: With me.

JACINTA: Take care of what you do!

COMMANDER: I do take care, and much the worse for you.
  No longer do I want you for myself,
  So you shall be the common property
  Of all my men.

JACINTA: No earthly power shall—
  While yet I draw my breath—degrade me thus!

COMMANDER: Come on, you peasant wench; get moving, there.

JACINTA: Have pity on me, sire!

COMMANDER: There's no such thing.

JACINTA: Against your cruelty's oppressive heel
  To Heaven's justice I make my appeal!

                    (*Jacinta is dragged off. Exeunt omnes*)

SCENE 12

A street in Fuente Ovejuna

Enter Laurencia and Frondoso

LAURENCIA: How do you dare to come here, risking death?

FRONDOSO: Ha sido
    dar testimonio cumplido
    de la afición que me debes.
    Desde aquel recuesto vi
    salir al Comendador,
    y fiado en tu valor
    todo mi temor perdí.
    ¡Vaya donde no le vean
    volver!

LAURENCIA: Tente en maldecir,
    porque suele más vivir
    al que la muerte desean.

FRONDOSO: Si es eso, viva mil años,
    y así se hará todo bien,
    pues deseándole bien,
    estarán ciertos sus daños.
    Laurencia, deseo saber
    si vive en ti mi cuidado,
    y si mi lealtad ha hallado
    el puerto de merecer.
    Mira que toda la villa
    ya para en uno nos tiene;
    y de cómo a ser no viene
    la villa se maravilla.
    Los desdeñosos extremos
    deja, y responde no o sí.

LAURENCIA: Pues a la villa y a ti
    respondo que lo seremos.

FRONDOSO: Deja que tus plantas bese
    por la merced recibida,
    pues el cobrar nueva vida
    por ella es bien que confiese.

LAURENCIA: De cumplimientos acorta;
    y para que mejor cuadre,
    habla, Frondoso, a mi padre,
    pues es lo que más importa,
    que allí viene con mi tío;
    y fía que ha de tener,
    ser, Frondoso, tu mujer,
    buen suceso.

FRONDOSO: The more to prove my deathless love for you.
From yonder hill I saw Commander Don
Fernán depart; inspired by your pluck,
I've lost all fear. May he be gone upon
A trip from which he never will return!

LAURENCIA: Don't curse him: those whose death we most desire
Live on until a ripe old age, it seems.

FRONDOSO: If so, then may he live a thousand years—
And that should settle him, for if we wish
Him well he will most surely come to grief.
Laurencia, I should like to know if you
Do care for me, and if my faithful bark
Of love has reached safe harbor in your heart.
The whole town looks upon us two as one,
And wonders why it is we do not wed.
Leave off your coy aloofness now, I pray,
And answer whether it be yea or nay.

LAURENCIA: Well then, my answer now were better said
To you and to the town: we shall be wed.
FRONDOSO: Laurencia, let me kiss your very feet
For this great boon that you have granted me.
Through this, I must confess, I have received
A brand new lease on life . . .
LAURENCIA: Now please cut short
Your compliments, Frondoso dear, and do
What is more fitting and important now:
Speak to my father. Here he comes, and with
Him is my uncle. Rest assured that ours
Will be a happy marriage, never fear.

FRONDOSO: En Dios confío.

(Entrase Laurencia en su casa)

ESCENA 13

Salen Esteban y el Regidor. Escóndese Frondoso

ESTEBAN: Fué su término de modo,
que la plaza alborotó:
en efecto, procedió
muy descomedido en todo.
No hay a quien admiración
sus demasías no den;
la pobre Jacinta es quien
pierde por su sinrazón.

REGIDOR: Ya a los Católicos Reyes,
que este nombre les dan ya,
presto España les dará
la obediencia de sus leyes.
Ya sobre Ciudad Real,
contra el Girón que la tiene,
Santiago a caballo viene
por capitán general.
Pésame; que era Jacinta
doncella de buena pro.

ESTEBAN: Luego a Mengo le azotó.

REGIDOR: No hay negra bayeta o tinta
como sus carnes están.

ESTEBAN: Callad; que me siento arder
viendo su mal proceder
y el mal nombre que le dan.
Yo ¿para qué traigo aquí
este palo sin provecho?

REGIDOR: Si sus criados lo han hecho
¿de qué os afligís ansí?

ESTEBAN: ¿Queréis más, que me contaron
que a la de Pedro Redondo
un día, que en lo más hondo
deste valle la encontraron,
después de sus insolencias,
a sus criados la dió?

FRONDOSO: I put my trust in God, Laurencia dear.

(*Laurencia goes into her house*)

SCENE 13

Enter Esteban and a Councilman. Frondoso takes cover

ESTEBAN: The matter ended thus: His actions, so
　　Despotic and high-handed, almost caused
　　A riot in the square. There is no one
　　Who is not stunned by his excesses; poor
　　Jacinta is the one who's had to pay
　　The price for his mad conduct here today.

COUNCILMAN: Soon now all Spaniards will obey the laws
　　Of Their Most Catholic Majesties—for such
　　The people are already calling them.
　　The Master of Santiago even now
　　Is riding as their Captain General
　　To Ciudad Real to wrest it from
　　Rodrigo of Girón, who holds it fast.
　　When I heard of Jacinta my heart bled,
　　For she's a modest maiden, and well-bred.

ESTEBAN: And then he ordered Mengo to be flogged.
COUNCILMAN: His flesh bears livid welts as dark as death.

ESTEBAN: No more! I feel my blood begin to boil
　　When I behold his foul, outrageous deeds
　　And hear the people curse his evil name.
　　I am the Mayor, but of what avail
　　Is this official staff I carry here?
COUNCILMAN: It was his servants did it; why should you
　　Distress yourself this way?
ESTEBAN:　　　　　　　　　You want more facts?
　　I'm told that after he had satisfied
　　His lust upon Redondo's wife one day
　　He passed her to his servants; she was found
　　Here at the bottom of this very glen.

REGIDOR: Aquí hay gente: ¿quién es?

FRONDOSO: Yo,
   que espero vuestras licencias.

ESTEBAN: Para mi casa, Frondoso,
   licencia no es menester;
   debes a tu padre el ser
   y a mí otro ser amoroso.
   Hete criado, y te quiero
   como a hijo.

FRONDOSO: Pues señor,
   fiado en aquese amor,
   de ti una merced espero.
   Ya sabes de quién soy hijo.

ESTEBAN: ¿Hate agraviado ese loco
   de Fernán Gómez?

FRONDOSO: No poco.

ESTEBAN: El corazón me lo dijo.

FRONDOSO: Pues señor, con el seguro
   del amor que habéis mostrado,
   de Laurencia enamorado,
   el ser su esposo procuro.
   Perdona si en el pedir
   mi lengua se ha adelantado;
   que he sido en decirlo osado,
   como otro lo ha de decir.

ESTEBAN: Vienes, Frondoso, a ocasión
   que me alargarás la vida,
   por la cosa más temida
   que siente mi corazón.
   Agradezco, hijo, al cielo
   que así vuelvas por mi honor
   y agradézcole a tu amor
   la limpieza de tu celo.
   Mas como es justo, es razón
   dar cuenta a tu padre desto;[1]
   sólo digo que estoy presto,
   en sabiendo su intención;
   que yo dichoso me hallo
   en que aqueso llegue a ser.

[1] *desto*   de esto

COUNCILMAN: There's someone lurking! Who is that?
FRONDOSO: It's me,
  Awaiting your permission to go in.
ESTEBAN: To go inside my house you do not need
  Permission, good Frondoso; you may owe
  Your being to your father, but to me
  (Since I have brought you up) you are as dear
  As if you were my own beloved son.

FRONDOSO: Well then, sir, trusting in your love for me,
  I beg a boon. You know whose son I am . . .

ESTEBAN: Has that mad Gómez done some wrong to you?

FRONDOSO: A great one, yes.
ESTEBAN: I knew it in my heart.
FRONDOSO: Sir, trusting in the love you've shown for me,
  I beg the hand of your Laurencia, whom
  I love. Forgive me if my tongue seems bold
  Or forward (as they say) in asking this.

ESTEBAN: Frondoso, your glad words give me new life,
  For at a time like this they help relieve
  The frightful fear that weighs upon my heart.
  My son, I give my thanks to Heaven for
  The fine concern you show for me and mine,
  And for the wholesome zeal of your pure love.
  But it is only right that you inform
  Your father of this plan; just let him know
  That I consent, if he is of like mind.
  I shall be glad to see this come to pass.

REGIDOR: De la moza el parecer
tomad antes de acetallo.[1]

ESTEBAN: No tengáis deso cuidado,
que ya el caso está dispuesto:
antes de venir a esto,
entre ellos se ha concertado.

(*A Frondoso*)

En el dote, si advertís,
se puede ahora tratar;
que por bien os pienso dar
algunos maravedís.

FRONDOSO: Yo dote no he menester;
deso no hay que entristeceros.

REGIDOR: Pues que no la pide en cueros
lo podéis agradecer.

ESTEBAN: Tomar el parecer della,
si os parece, será bien.

FRONDOSO: Justo es; que no hace bien
quien los gustos atropella.

ESTEBAN (*Llamando*): ¡Hija! ¡Laurencia! . . .

ESCENA 14

Laurencia, saliendo de su casa

LAURENCIA: Señor . . .

ESTEBAN (*Al Regidor*): Mirad si digo bien yo.
¡Ved qué presto respondió!
Hija Laurencia, mi amor,
a preguntarte ha venido
(apártate aquí) si es bien
que a Gila, tu amiga, den
a Frondoso por marido,
que es un honrado zagal,
si le hay en Fuenteovejuna . . .

---

[1] *acetallo*   aceptarlo

COUNCILMAN: Before accepting him you ought to get
　　The girl's opinion first.

ESTEBAN:　　　　　　　　Please do not fret
　　About that point: they had it all arranged
　　Between themselves before he spoke to me!

(*To Frondoso*)

　　As for the dowry, we can talk of that
　　Right now, if you've a mind; I plan to give
　　You two a little sum I've set aside.

FRONDOSO: I need no dowry, sir; please do not put
　　Yourself to any trouble on that score.

COUNCILMAN: He takes her as she is: you should be glad.

ESTEBAN: If you don't mind, I'll ask her what she thinks.

FRONDOSO: That's proper. To oppose her will in this
　　Would not be right.

ESTEBAN (*Calling*):　　　Laurencia! Daughter! Come!

SCENE 14

Laurencia comes out of her house

LAURENCIA: Yes, Father?

ESTEBAN (*Aside*):　　　(Look how quickly she replied!
　　You see how right I was?). Laurencia, dear,
　　I want to ask you if you feel it's right
　　That your friend Gila should be married to
　　Frondoso, who is quite the finest lad
　　There is in Fuente Ovejuna. Come!

LAURENCIA: ¿Gila se casa?

ESTEBAN: Y si alguna
le merece y es su igual . . .

LAURENCIA: Yo digo, señor, que sí.

ESTEBAN: Sí; mas yo digo que es fea
y que harto mejor se emplea
Frondoso, Laurencia, en ti.

LAURENCIA: ¿Aún no se te han olvidado
los donaires con la edad?

ESTEBAN: ¿Quiéresle tú?

LAURENCIA: Voluntad
le he tenido y le he cobrado;
pero por lo que tú sabes . . .

ESTEBAN: ¿Quires tú que diga sí?

LAURENCIA: Dilo tú, señor, por mí.

ESTEBAN (*Al Regidor*): Yo? Pues tengo yo las llaves,
hecho está. Ven, buscaremos
a mi compadre en la plaza.

REGIDOR: Vamos.

ESTEBAN (*a Frondoso*): Hijo, y en la traza
del dote ¿qué le diremos?
Que yo bien te puedo dar
cuatro mil maravedís.

FRONDOSO: Señor, ¿eso me decís?
Mi honor queréis agraviar.

ESTEBAN: Anda, hijo; que eso es
cosa que pasa en un día;
que si no hay dote, a fe mía,
que se echa menos después.

(*Vanse, y quedan Frondoso y Laurencia*)

LAURENCIA: Di, Frondoso: ¿estás contento?

FRONDOSO: ¡Cómo si lo estoy! ¡Es poco,
pues que no me vuelvo loco
de gozo, del bien que siento!
Risa vierte el corazón
por los ojos, de alegría
viéndote, Laurencia mía,
en tal dulce posesión.

(*Vanse*)

LAURENCIA: Is Gila getting married?

ESTEBAN: If there is
A girl deserves him, she's a worthy match.

LAURENCIA: Yes, Father, I agree.

ESTEBAN: I'd say the same,
But she is ugly and I think that he
Would do much better to be courting you.

LAURENCIA: In spite of all your years you haven't yet
Forgotten how to compliment a girl!

ESTEBAN: But aren't you in love with him yourself?

LAURENCIA: I've come to be quite fond of him, it's true,
But now this Gila business has come up . . .

ESTEBAN: So you do want me to say yes to him?

LAURENCIA: Please say it for me, Father; tell him yes!

ESTEBAN (*To Councilman*):
Since I'm the one who holds the key to this,
It's settled, then. Now let us go and find
Frondoso's father in the square.

COUNCILMAN: Let's go!

ESTEBAN (*To Frondoso*): My boy, what shall we say to him about
This matter of the dowry? I can well
Afford to give you quite a tidy sum . . .

FRONDOSO: But, sir, why bring that up? You wound my pride.

ESTEBAN: Come, come, my son; you'll soon get over that;
You'll need the dowry later on, I'm sure.

(*Exeunt Esteban and the Councilman*)

LAURENCIA: Frondoso, tell me: are you happy, dear?

FRONDOSO: Indeed I am! I'm almost going mad
With all the joy and happiness I feel.
My laughing heart brims from my eyes like wine,
Laurencia, when I think you'll soon be mine.

(*Exeunt Laurencia and Frondoso*)

ESCENA 15

Campo de Ciudad Real

Salen el Maestre, el Comendador, Flores
y Ortuño; soldados

COMENDADOR: Huye, señor, que no hay otro remedio.

MAESTRE: La flaqueza del muro lo ha causado,
y el poderoso ejército enemigo.

COMENDADOR: Sangre les cuesta e infinitas vidas.

MAESTRE: Y no se alabarán, que en sus despojos
pondrán nuestro pendón de Calatrava,
que a honrar su empresa y los demás bastaba.

COMENDADOR: Tus designios, Girón, quedan perdidos.

MAESTRE: ¿Qué puedo hacer, si la fortuna ciega
a quien hoy levantó, mañana humilla?

VOCES (*dentro*): ¡Victoria por los reyes de Castilla!

MAESTRE: Ya coronan de luces las almenas,
y las ventanas de las torres altas
entoldan con pendones victoriosos.

COMENDADOR: Bien pudieran de sangre que les cuesta.
A fe que es más tragedia que no fiesta.

MAESTRA: Yo vuelvo a Calatrava, Fernán Gómez.

COMENDADOR: Y yo a Fuenteovejuna, mientras tratas
o seguir esta parte de tus deudos,
o reducir la tuya al Rey Católico.

MAESTRE: Yo te diré por cartas lo que intento.

COMENDADOR: El tiempo ha de enseñarte.

MAESTRE: ¡Ah, pocos años,
sujetos al rigor de sus engaños!

(*Vanse todos*)

SCENE 15

The countryside near Ciudad Real

Enter the Master of Calatrava, the Commander,
Flores and Ortuño, accompanied by soldiers

COMMANDER: Flee, Don Rodrigo! It's our only hope!

MASTER: The weakness of the rampart was the cause,
Along with the opposing army's strength.

COMMANDER: It cost them blood enough, and many lives.

MASTER: At least they cannot boast that they have seized
Our flag of Calatrava with the spoils;
They will not add that honor to their arms!

COMMANDER: But even so, Girón, your hopes are lost.

MASTER: What can I do if Fortune's blind, and vexed?
My hopes were raised one day, and crushed the next.

(*Voices are heard offstage*)

VOICES: It's victory! Hail, Monarchs of Castile!

MASTER: The battlements are crowned with victor lights,
And from the tower windows there on high
The banners of the conquerors now fly.

COMMANDER: Their flags might better be red-tinged with blood,
For it is more a tragedy, I vow,
Than celebration.

MASTER: I shall now return
To Calatrava, Don Fernán. And you?

COMMANDER: I'm off to Fuente Ovejuna while
You follow up your kinsmen's cause, or else
Decide to join King Ferdinand in his.

MASTER: I'll let you know by letter what I plan.

COMMANDER: Yes, time alone will show you what is best.

MASTER: To be so young, yet face this bitter test!

(*Exeunt omnes*)

ESCENA 16

Campo de Fuenteovejuna

Sale la boda, músicos, Mengo, Frondoso, Laurencia,
Pascuala, Barrildo, Esteban y Juan Rojo

MÚSICOS (*Cantan*): *¡Vivan muchos años*
los desposados!
¡Vivan muchos años!

MENGO: A fe que no os ha costado
mucho trabajo el cantar.

BARRILDO: Supiéraslo tú trovar
mejor que él está trovado.

FRONDOSO: Mejer entiende de azotes
Mengo que de versos ya.

MENGO: Alguno en el valle está,
para que no te alborotes,
a quien el Comendador . . .

BARRILDO: No lo digas, por tu vida;
que este bárbaro homicida
a todos quita el honor.

MENGO: Que me azotasen a mí
cien soldados aquel día . . .
sola una honda tenía;
pero que le hayan echado
una melecina[1] a un hombre,
que aunque no diré su nombre
todos saben que es honrado,
llena de tinta y de chinas
¿cómo se puede sufrir?

BARRILDO: Haríalo por reír.

MENGO: No hay risa con melecinas;
que aunque es cosa saludable . . .
yo me quiero morir luego.

FRONDOSO: Vaya la copla, te ruego,
si es la copla razonable.

---

[1] *melecina*   medicina (lavativa)

SCENE 16

The countryside near Fuente Ovejuna

Enter Mengo, Frondoso, Laurencia, Pascuala,
Barrildo, Juan Rojo, Esteban, wedding guests,
and musicians

MUSICIANS (*Singing*): Long live the new-wed man and wife!
May they enjoy a good long life!

MENGO: Upon my faith, you didn't have to work
Too hard on that!
BARRILDO: Well, Mengo, let's hear you
Compose a better song than that one is.
FRONDOSO: Poor Mengo now knows more about a whip
Than verses.
MENGO: In the valley there is one
Can stop your jesting—the Commander, and . . .

BARRILDO: Don't mention his foul name, for Heaven's sake!
That murderer dishonors all of us.

MENGO: That day there were a hundred men to one,
And I had but a sling: they flogged me hard.
But better that than be the man to whom
They gave an enema of dye and herbs—
An honest fellow, whom I shall not name.
How could he stand it!

BARRILDO: They did it for laughs.
MENGO: A dose like that is not a cause for mirth.
Although an enema's a healthful thing,
I'd rather die right off than suffer that!
FRONDOSO: Let's hear your poem, if it's any good.

MENGO: Vivan muchos años juntos
  los novios, ruego a los cielos,
  y por envidia ni celos
  ni riñan ni anden en puntos.
  Lleven a entrambos difuntos,
  de puro vivir cansados.
  ¡Vivan muchos años!

FRONDOSO: ¡Maldiga el cielo el poeta,
  que tal coplón arrojó!

BARRILDO: Fué muy presto . . .

MENGO: Pienso yo
  una cosa de esta seta.[1]
  ¿No habéis visto un buñolero
  en el aceite abrasando
  pedazos de masa echando
  hasta llenarse el caldero?
  ¿Que unos le salen hinchados,
  otros tuertos y mal hechos,
  ya zurdos y ya derechos,
  ya fritos y ya quemados?
  Pues así imagino yo
  un poeta componiendo,
  la materia previniendo,
  que es quien la masa le dió.
  Va arrojando verso aprisa
  al caldero del papel,
  confiado en que la miel
  cubrirá la burla y risa.
  Mas poniéndolo en el pecho,
  apenas hay quien los tome;
  tanto que sólo los come
  el mismo que los ha hecho.

BARRILDO: Déjate ya de locuras;
  deja los novios hablar.

LAURENCIA: Las manos nos da a besar.

JUAN ROJO: Hija, ¿mi mano procuras?
  Pídela a tu padre luego
  para ti ya para Frondoso.

[1] *seta*   secta

MENGO (*Reciting*): I pray to Heaven up above
That these two newlyweds in love
May live for years.
May envy and may jealous strife
Stay far from their long wedded life,
And cause no tears.
When they have tired of life's long stay
May they be carried both away
Upon twin biers.

FRONDOSO: May Heaven curse the poet who tossed off
Such rotten verses!

BARRILDO: But the time was short . . .

MENGO: Here's what I think about the poet's craft.
You've seen a doughnut-maker throw some dough
Into the bubbling oil until the pan
Is full? Some come out all puffed up, and some
Are twisted to the right or to the left,
While some turn out well-fried and others burnt.
Well, that is how I think a poet works
When he composes, using his ideas
The way the baker handles dough: he drops
His verses in the literary pot
And trusts the sugar coating will conceal
Some aspects that are really ludicrous.
But when he puts them up for sale he finds
That there is hardly anyone who cares,
So he himself consumes his half-baked wares.

BARRILDO: Leave off such madness; let the lovers speak.

LAURENCIA: Give us your hands to kiss in gratitude.

ROJO: Dear girl, you seek my hand? 'Twere better that
You two should ask to kiss your father's first.

ESTEBAN: Rojo, a ella y a su esposo
que se la dé el cielo ruego,
con su larga bendición.

FRONDOSO: Los dos a los dos la echad.

JUAN ROJO: Ea, tañed y cantad,
pues que para en uno son.

MÚSICOS (*Cantan*): *Al val de Fuenteovejuna*
la niña en cabellos baja;
el caballero la sigue
de la cruz de Calatrava.
Entre las ramas se esconde,
de vergonzosa y turbada;
fingiendo que no le ha visto,
pone delante las ramas.
"¿Para qué te escondes,
niña gallarda?
Que mis linces deseos
paredes pasan".
Acercóse el caballero,
y ella, confusa y turbada,
hacer quiso celosías
de las intrincadas ramas;
mas como quien tiene amor
los mares y las montañas
atraviesa fácilmente,
la dice tales palabras:
"¿Para qué te escondes,
niña gallarda?
Que mis linces deseos
paredes pasan".

(*Dejan de cantar*)

ESTEBAN: My only wish, dear Rojo, for my girl
  And for her husband is that Heaven grant
  Unending blessings to the two of them.

FRONDOSO: We beg that both of you bless both of us.

ROJO: Musicians, let us hear you sing and play,
  To celebrate their union here this day.

MUSICIANS (*Singing*):
      The maiden goes down to the valley,
      With her hair flowing free in the breeze;
      Calatrava's bold knight make a sally,
      And the Cross on his doublet she sees.
      Among the thick branches she plunges
      To conceal her confusion and fear;
      The knight through the brush onward lunges
      And she feigns not to see him so near.

    Why are you hiding, maiden fair?
      My ardor is so keen
    That my lynx-eyes can see you there
      For they pierce any screen.

      The knight comes up close to the maiden,
      So she fashions a cover of green
      Where, perturbed and with heart heavy laden,
      She shrinks down lest her beauty be seen.
      In the chase, 'tis but play for a wooer
      To traverse mighty mountains and seas;
      Through the thicket he seeks to pursue her
      And to woo her with words such as these:

    Why are you hiding, maiden fair?
      My ardor is so keen
    That my lynx-eyes can see you there,
      For they pierce any screen.

                    (*The musicians suddenly stop singing*)

ESCENA 17

Sale el Comendador, Flores, Ortuño y
Cimbranos; soldados

COMENDADOR: Estése la boda queda
y no se alborote nadie.

JUAN ROJO: No es juego aqueste, señor,
y basta que tú lo mandes.
¿Quieres lugar? ¿Cómo vienes
con tu belicoso alarde?
¿Venciste? Mas ¿qué pregunto?

FRONDOSO (*aparte*): ¡Muerto soy! ¡Cielos, libradme!

LAURENCIA: Huye por aquí, Frondoso.

COMENDADOR: Eso no; prendedle, atadle.

JUAN ROJO: Date, muchacho, a prisión.

FRONDOSO: Pues ¿quieres tú que me maten?

JUAN ROJO: ¿Por qué?

COMENDADOR: No soy hombre yo
que mato sin culpa a nadie;
que si lo fuera, le hubieran
pasado de parte a parte
esos soldados que traigo.
Llevarle mando a la cárcel,
donde la culpa que tiene
sentencie su mismo padre.

PASCUALA: Señor, mirad que se casa.

COMENDADOR: ¿Qué me obliga el que se case?
¿No hay otra gente en el pueblo?

PASCUALA: Si os ofendió perdonadle,
por ser vos quien sois.

COMENDADOR: No es cosa,
Pascuala, en que yo soy parte.
Es esto contra el maestre
Tellez Girón, que Dios guarde;
es contra toda su orden,
es su honor, y es importante
para el ejemplo, el castigo;

SCENE 17

*Enter the Commander, Flores, Ortuño, and
Cimbranos, accompanied by soldiers*

COMMANDER: Let no one be upset on my account,
Continue with your wedding games, I pray.

ROJO: This is no game, my lord; your slightest wish
Is our command, however. Please sit down.
But why the full accoutrements of war?
You're fresh from victory? But then, why ask?

FRONDOSO (*Aside*): I am undone! May Heaven help me now!

LAURENCIA: Frondoso, run! This way!

COMMANDER: No! Seize him, men,
And tie him up!

ROJO: You must surrender, lad.

FRONDOSO: You want them all to kill me, then?

ROJO: But why?

COMMANDER: I'm not a man who kills without just cause;
If that were so, my soldiers would have run
Him through by this time. I now order them
To take him off to jail; his father there
Shall try his guilt and mete out punishment.

PASCUALA: But sire, he's just been married, as you see.

COMMANDER: He's just been married? What is that to me?
Is he the only person here in town?

PASCUALA: If he offended you, forgive him, sire.
Noblesse oblige.

COMMANDER: Pascuala, I am not
The one concerned in this affair at all.
The one offended is Téllez Girón
(May God preserve him); the affair involves
The Master, and our Order's honor, too.
It is important that the punishment

que habrá otro día quien trate
de alzar pendón contra él,
pues ya sabéis que una tarde
al Comendador Mayor
(¡qué vasallos tan leales!)
puso una ballesta al pecho.

ESTEBAN: Supuesto que el disculparle
ya puede tocar a un suegro,
no es mucho que en causas tales
se descomponga con vos
un hombre, en efecto, amante;
porque si vos pretendéis
su propia mujer quitarle,
¿qué mucho que la defienda?

COMENDADOR: Majadero sois, alcalde.

ESTEBAN: Por vuestra virtud, señor.

COMENDADOR: Nunca yo quise quitarle
su mujer, pues no lo era.

ESTEBAN: Sí quisisteis . . . Y esto baste;
que reyes hay en Castilla,
que nuevas órdenes hacen,
con que desórdenes quitan.
Y harán mal, cuando descansen
de las guerras, en sufrir
en sus villas y lugares
a hombres tan poderosos
por traer cruces tan grandes;
póngasela el rey al pecho,
que para pechos reales
es esa insignia y no más.

COMENDADOR: ¡Hola! la vara quitadle.

ESTEBAN: Tomad, señor norabuena.

COMENDADOR: Pues con ella quiero darle
como a caballo brioso.

ESTEBAN: Por señor os sufro. Dadme.

PASCUALA: ¡A un viejo de palos das!

LAURENCIA: Si le das porque es mi padre
¿qué vengas en él de mí?

Frondoso will receive should serve to warn
All others who might some day seek to rise
Against the rule of our Grand Master, for
You know that this young man one afternoon
(What loyal subjects!) aimed a crossbow at
The breast of a Commander.

ESTEBAN: If it be
Not out of place for me to plead for my
New son-in-law, then I would say that in
A case like this is it so strange, indeed,
That any man—a husband, almost—should
Be moved to anger when you seek to take
Away his bride, and come to her defense?

COMMANDER: Mayor Esteban, you're a meddling fool!
ESTEBAN: But it is for your virtue's sake, my lord.
COMMANDER: I never wished to take away his bride:
    They weren't married yet.
ESTEBAN: You wanted to . . .
But that's enough. There are now in Castile
A King and Queen to promulgate new laws,
And with them such abuses soon will cease.
They will not rest upon their laurels when
The wars are won; in villages and towns
No man will be allowed to hold such sway
Because he wears the Calatrava Cross.
The King alone is worthy of that crest:
Let good Fernando wear it on his breast!

COMMANDER: Ho! Snatch that staff of office from his hands!
ESTEBAN: Pray take it, sire; I yield it willingly.
COMMANDER: I'll beat him with it, like a balky horse.

ESTEBAN: I yield: you are my master. Strike me, then.
PASCUALA: Would you descend to beating an old man?
LAURENCIA: But how do you revenge yourself on me
    By beating him? Because I am his child?

COMENDADOR: Llevadla, y haced que guarden
su persona diez soldados.

(Vanse él y los suyos llevándose presos a Laurencia
y Frondoso)

ESTEBAN: ¡Justicia del cielo baje!

(Vase)

PASCUALA: Volvióse en luto la boda.

(Vase)

BARRILDO: ¿No hay aquí un hombre que hable?

MENGO: Yo tengo ya mis azotes,
que aun se ven los cardenales
sin que un hombre vaya a Roma.
Prueben otros a enojarle.

JUAN ROJO: Hablemos todos.

MENGO: Señores, aquí todo el mundo calle.
Como ruedas de salmón
me puso los atabales[1]!

(Vanse todos)

---

[1] *atabales*   nalgas

COMMANDER: Arrest that girl; let ten men guard her well.

> *(The Commander leaves with his men, who are*
> *leading Frondoso and Laurencia as prisoners)*

ESTEBAN: May Heaven send its justice down on him!

> *(Exit Esteban)*

PASCUALA: The wedding has become a time to mourn.

> *(Exit Pascuala)*

BARRILDO: Is there no man among us who will speak?

MENGO: Let someone else speak out and rile him up.
From being whipped I am as purple as
A cardinal—without a trip to Rome!

ROJO: Let's all speak up together.

MENGO: Gentlemen,
Let's all be silent here, for Heaven's sake:
He's flogged me so I'm red as salmon steak!

> *(Exeunt omnes)*

ACTO TERCERO

❦

ESCENA 1

Sala del Concejo en Fuenteovejuna

Salen Esteban, Alonso y Barrildo

ESTEBAN: ¿No han venido a la junta?

BARRILDO: No han venido.

ESTEBAN: Pues más aprisa nuestro daño corre.

BARRILDO: Ya está lo más del pueblo prevenido.

ESTEBAN: Frondoso con prisiones en la torre,
y mi hija Laurencia en tanto aprieto,
si la piedad de Dios no los socorre . . .

ESCENA 2

Salen Juan Rojo y el Regidor. Después, Mengo

JUAN ROJO: ¿De qué dais voces, cuando importa tanto
a nuestro bien, Esteban, el secreto?

ESTEBAN: Que doy tan pocas es mayor espanto.

MENGO: También yo vengo a hallarme en esta junta.

ESTEBAN: Un hombre cuyas canas baña el llanto,
labradores honrados, os pregunta
qué obsequias debe hacer toda esa gente
a su patria sin honra, ya perdida.
Y si se llaman honras justamente,
¿cómo se harán, si no hay entre nosotros
hombre a quien este bárbaro no afrente?

ACT THREE

SCENE 1

The Council Chamber in Fuente Ovejuna

Enter Esteban, Alonso, and Barrildo

ESTEBAN: Have they not come to meet with us?

BARRILDO: Not yet.

ESTEBAN: Our danger, then, grows greater as we wait.

BARRILDO: Most everyone in town has been informed.

ESTEBAN: With good Frondoso in the tower jail,
  And my Laurencia in great danger, too,
  If God's great mercy does not help them, then . . .

SCENE 2

*Enter Juan Rojo and the Councilman,
followed by Mengo*

ROJO: Why shout like that, Esteban, when you know
  That secrecy is vital to our cause?

ESTEBAN: The wonder is that I'm not shouting more.

MENGO (*Entering*): I, too, would like to join this meeting here.

ESTEBAN: A man whose graying beard is bathed in tears
  Asks you, my honest farmers, how our folk
  Should mourn the death of honor in this land.
  What use to mourn our vanished honor now,
  If there is not a man among us who
  Is not degraded by this evil fiend?

Respondedme: ¿hay alguno de vosotros
que no esté lastimado en honra y vida?
¿No os lamentáis los unos de los otros?
Pues si ya la tenéis todos perdida
¿a qué aguardáis? ¿Qué desventura es ésta?

JUAN ROJO: La mayor que en el mundo fué sufrida.
Mas pues ya se publica y manifiesta
que en paz tienen los reyes a Castilla
y su venida a Córdoba se apresta,
vayan dos regidores a la villa
y echándose a sus pies pidan remedio.

BARRILDO: En tanto que Fernando al suelo humilla
a tantos enemigos, otro medio
será mejor, pues no podrá, ocupado,
hacernos bien, con tanta guerra en medio.

REGIDOR: Si mi voto de vos fuera escuchado,
desamparar la villa doy por voto.

JUAN ROJO: ¿Cómo es posible en tiempo limitado?

MENGO: A la fe, que si entiende el alboroto,
que ha de costar la junta alguna vida.

REGIDOR: Ya, todo el árbol de paciencia roto,
corre la nave de temor perdida.
La hija quitan con tan gran fiereza
a un hombre honrado, de quien es regida
la patria en que vivís, y en la cabeza
la vara quiebran tan injustamente.
¿Qué esclavo se trató con más bajeza?

JUAN ROJO: ¿Qué es lo que quieres tú que el pueblo intente?

REGIDOR: Morir, o dar la muerte a los tiranos,
pues somos muchos, y ellos poca gente.

BARRILDO: ¡Contra el señor las armas en las manos!

ESTEBAN: El rey sólo es señor después del cielo,
y no bárbaros hombres inhumanos.
Si Dios ayuda nuestro justo celo
¿qué nos ha de costar?

Just answer me: is there among you one
Who has not been sore wounded in his soul
And deepest dignity? Do you not weep
For one another? If you all have lost
Your very honor, then why hesitate?
What worse could now befall, at this late date?

ROJO: The worst misfortune that this world has seen!
But there is news about the King and Queen:
'Tis known that they have pacified Castile,
And shortly will appear in Córdoba.
Two councilmen should journey to that town
And kneel before them, asking for their aid.

BARRILDO: Some other method must be found; the King
Is fully occupied in putting down
A host of enemies, and cannot help
Us now while in the midst of waging war.

COUNCILMAN: If you would hear my voice, my vote would be
That we should all evacuate this town.

ROJO: How could we do that in so short a time?

MENGO: Upon my faith, if anyone should hear
The noise this council's making it will cost
A life or two among us!

COUNCILMAN: Now the mast
Of patience has been shattered and our ship
Of state drives on, the helpless prey of fear.
They fiercely snatch away the daughter of
The honest man who governs in this town
In which you live, and break his very staff
Of office cruelly upon his head.
What slave was ever vilely treated thus?

ROJO: What is it that you want the town to do?

COUNCILMAN: To die—or else to deal those tyrants death:
For we are many, and they are but few.

BARRILDO: To take up arms against our rightful lord?

ESTEBAN: The King alone is rightfully our lord—
Right after God—and not these barbarous,
Inhuman men. If God is aiding us
In our just cause, what have we then to fear?

MENGO: Mirad, señores,
que vais[1] en estas cosas con recelo.
Puesto que por los simples labradores
estoy aquí que más injurias pasan,
más cuerdo represento sus temores.

JUAN ROJO: Si nuestras desventuras se compasan,
para perder las vidas, ¿qué aguardamos?
Las casas y las viñas nos abrasan:
Tiranos son; a la venganza vamos.

ESCENA 3

Sale Laurencia, desmelenada

LAURENCIA: Dejadme entrar, que bien puedo,
en consejo de los hombres;
que bien puede una mujer,
si no a dar voto, a dar voces.
¿Conocéisme?

ESTEBAN: ¡Santo cielo!
¿No es mi hija?

JUAN ROJO: ¿No conoces
a Laurencia?

LAURENCIA: Vengo tal,
que mi diferencia os pone
en contingencia quién soy.

ESTEBAN: ¡Hija mía!

LAURENCIA: No me nombres
tu hija.

ESTEBAN: ¿Por qué, mis ojos?
¿Por qué?

LAURENCIA: Por muchas razones,
y sean las principales:
porque dejas que me roben
tiranos sin que me vengues,
traidores sin que me cobres.

[1] *vais*   vayáis

MENGO: But look you, gentlemen: be cautious now
In matters such as these. I represent
The simple farmers here—who suffer most—
And I can best express their rightful fears.

ROJO: If we have borne affronts like these until
Our lives are meaningless, then why wait more?
These tyrants burn our homes, and vineyards, too:
Now let us act! Revenge is overdue!

SCENE 3

Enter Laurencia, all dishevelled

LAURENCIA: Let me inside! A woman has a right
At least to have a voice—if not a vote—
Among you men in council gathered here.
Do you know who I am?

ESTEBAN:　　　　　　　Good God above!
Is this my daughter?
ROJO:　　　　　　　Don't you know your own
Laurencia?
LAURENCIA:　　　I am now in such a state
You may not recognize just who I am.

ESTEBAN: Dear daughter!
LAURENCIA:　　　　　　　Call me that no longer, please.

ESTEBAN: But why, my darling girl? Just tell me why?

LAURENCIA: For many reasons, chief among them these:
You let those wretched tyrants take me off,
And still did not avenge or rescue me.

Aun no era yo de Frondoso,
para que digas que tome,
como marido, venganza;
que aquí por tu cuenta corre;
que en tanto que de las bodas
no haya llegado la noche,
del padre, y no del marido,
la obligación presupone;
que en tanto que no me entregan
una joya, aunque la compre,
no han de correr por mi cuenta
las guardas ni los ladrones.
Llevóme de vuestros ojos
a su casa Fernán Gómez:
la oveja al lobo dejáis
como cobardes pastores.
¿Qué dagas no vi en mi pecho?
¡Qué desatinos enormes,
qué palabras, qué amenazas,
y qué delitos atroces,
por rendir mi castidad
a sus apetitos torpes!
Mis cabellos ¿no lo dicen?
Las señales de los golpes
¿no se ven aquí, y la sangre?
¿Vosotros sois hombres nobles?
¿Vosotros padres y deudos?
¿Vosotros, que no se os rompen
las entrañas de dolor,
de verme en tantos dolores?
Ovejas sois, bien lo dice
de Fuenteovejuna el nombre.
Dadme unas armas a mí,
pues sois piedras, pues sois bronces,
pues sois jaspes, pues sois tigres . . .
Tigres no, porque feroces
siguen quien roba sus hijos,
matando los cazadores
antes que entren por el mar
y por sus ondas se arrojen.

I was not yet Frondoso's wife, so you
Ought not have felt that it was up to him,
My husband, to avenge me; it was your
Responsibility. The wedding night
Had not yet come: until that time one holds
The father—not the husband—duty bound;
When one has bought a gem, until such time
As it is handed over he is not
Responsible for guarding it from thieves.
Before your very eyes, you men all saw
Me dragged off to the house of Don Fernán;
You let a lamb be taken by a wolf,
As coward shepherds do. They set their knives
Against my breast! What filthy words they said,
What threats they made, what bestial tricks they tried,
To make me yield myself to his foul lust!
And don't you see my hair all torn? Look here
At these big, bloody bruises from their blows!
And do you call yourselves good, upright men?
Are you my relatives—my father, too—
Who look upon me thus in such travail
And do not burst with grief and righteous wrath?
You are just sheep! The very village name
Of Fuente Ovejuna means "a fount
Where sheep come for a drink"—and such are you!
Give me your weapons! You have hearts of stone
Or metal; you are paper tigers—no,
Not tigers: they at least protect their young
By tracking down ferociously the men
Who steal their cubs, and catch them long before
They reach their ships and put to sea again.

Liebres cobardes nacisteis;
bárbaros[1] sois, no españoles.
Gallinas, ¡vuestras mujeres
sufrís que otros hombres gocen!
Ponéos ruecas en la cinta.
¿Para qué os ceñís estoques?
¡Vive Dios, que he de trazar
que solas mujeres cobren
la honra destos tiranos,
la sangre destos traidores,
y que os han de tirar piedras,
hilanderas, maricones,
amujerados, cobardes,
y que mañana os adornen
nuestras tocas y basquiñas,
solimanes[2] y colores!
A Frondoso quiere ya,
sin sentencia, sin pregones,
colgar el Comendador
del almena de una torre;
de todos hará lo mismo;
y yo me huelgo, medio-hombres,
por que quede sin mujeres
esta villa honrada, y torne
aquel siglo de amazonas,
eterno espanto del orbe.

ESTEBAN: Yo, hija, no soy de aquellos
que permiten que los nombres
con esos títulos viles.
Iré solo, si se pone
todo el mundo contra mí.

JUAN ROJO: Y yo, por más que me asombre
la grandeza del contrario.

REGIDOR: Muramos todos.

---

[1] *bárbaros*   extranjeros

[2] *solimanes*   afeites

You've all been craven rabbits right from birth!
You are not Spanish men, but heathen slaves!
You cluck like chickens while you let your wives
And daughters be enjoyed by other men!
Put spindles in your belts instead of swords!
By God above, we women all alone
Will soon redeem our honor from these swine
And take their tyrant blood! And as for you,
You gabbing cowards, sissies, panty-waists,
We'll dress you up in petticoats and lace,
And you can wear our rouge and powder, too,
While we hurl stones and epithets at you!
Frondoso is about to be strung up
By Don Fernán right from the battlements
Without a legal sentence or appeal,
And he will do the same to all of you.
I'm glad of it, you half-men, so our town
Will thus be rid of all effeminates;
The Age of Amazons will have new birth,
And be the lasting wonder of this earth!

ESTEBAN: My girl, I am not one of those to whom
Those sordid words can properly apply;
I'll fight alone, and all the world defy!

ROJO: I fear the strength of our bold enemy,
But I shall go, and you can count on me!
COUNCILMAN: Let's all seek death together!

BARRILDO: Descoge[1]
un lienzo al viento en un palo,
y mueran estos inormes.[2]

JUAN ROJO: ¿Qué orden pensáis tener?

MENGO: Ir a matarle sin orden.
Juntad el pueblo a una voz;
que todos están conformes
en que los tiranos mueran.

ESTEBAN: Tomad espadas, lanzones,
ballestas, chuzos y palos.

MENGO: ¡Los reyes nuestros señores
vivan!

TODOS: ¡Vivan muchos años!

MENGO: ¡Mueran tiranos traidores!

TODOS: ¡Traidores tiranos mueran!

(Vanse todos los hombres)

LAURENCIA: Caminad, que el cielo os oye.

(Gritando)

¡Ah mujeres de la villa!
¡Acudid, por que se cobre
vuestro honor, acudid todas!

ESCENA 4

Salen Pascuala, Jacinta y otras mujeres

PASCUALA: ¿Qué es esto? ¿De qué das voces?

LAURENCIA: ¿No veis cómo todos van
a matar a Fernán Gómez,
y hombres, mozos y muchachos
furiosos al hecho corren?
¿Será bien que solos ellos
desta hazaña el honor gocen,
pues no son de las mujeres
sus agravios los menores?

JACINTA: Di, pues: ¿qué es lo que pretendes?

---

[1] *descoge*   despliega
[2] *inormes*   enormes

BARRILDO: We'll unfurl
  A cloth upon a pole, our banner brave,
  And send these monstrous tyrants to the grave!

ROJO: And what shall be the order of our march?

MENGO: We'll have no ordered march: just go and kill!
  Our folk will rally at a single cry,
  For all agree the tyrants now must die!

ESTEBAN: Bring swords and lances, bows and pikes and clubs!

MENGO: Long live the King and Queen, our sovereigns!

ALL: Long life to them!

MENGO: And death to tyrants vile!

ALL: May all vile tyrants die!

                        (*The men leave in a group*)

LAURENCIA (*Shouting*):   God speed your way . . .

  All women of this town, if you'd be free
  And would redeem your honor, come to me!

SCENE 4

Enter Pascuala and Jacinta, followed by other women

PASCUALA: What is all this? Why are you shouting so?

LAURENCIA: You see how men and youths, and even boys,
  Have gone to kill Commander Don Fernán,
  All seized with fury, rushing to the fray?
  Should only they gain glory from this deed
  When we, the women, suffer more than they?

JACINTA: Well, tell us then what you propose we do.

LAURENCIA: Que puestas todas en orden,
acometamos un hecho
que dé espanto a todo el orbe.
Jacinta, a tu grande agravio,
que seas cabo corresponde
de una escuadra de mujeres.

JACINTA: No son los tuyos menores.

LAURENCIA: Pascuala, alférez serás.

PASCUALA: Pues déjame que enarbole
en un asta la bandera:
verás si merezco el nombre.

LAURENCIA: No hay espacio para eso,
pues la dicha nos socorre:
bien nos basta que llevemos
nuestras tocas por pendones.

PASCUALA: Nombremos un capitán.

LAURENCIA: Eso no.

PASCUALA: ¿Por qué?

LAURENCIA: Que adonde
asiste mi gran valor
no hay Cides ni Rodamontes.

(Vanse)

ESCENA 5

Sala en casa del Comendador

*Sale Frondoso, atadas las manos; Flores, Ortuño,
Cimbranos y el Comendador*

COMENDADOR: De ese cordel que de las manos sobra
quiero que le colguéis, por mayor pena.

FRONDOSO: ¡Qué nombre, gran señor, tu sangre cobra!

COMENDADOR: Colgadle luego en la primera almena.

FRONDOSO: Nunca fué mi intención poner por obra
tu muerte entonces.

(Ruido)

LAURENCIA: We'll organize on military lines,
And do a deed that will amaze the world.
Jacinta, you have suffered monstrous wrongs,
So you shall be the leader of a squad.

JACINTA: The wrongs done you have been as great as mine.
LAURENCIA: Pascuala, you shall be our ensign bold.
PASCUALA: Just let me hold the flag on high, and you
Shall see that I deserve an ensign's rank.

LAURENCIA: There is no time for flags; we must move fast
While fate is on our side: our caps shall serve
As standards.

PASCUALA: Let us choose a captain now.
LAURENCIA: Not that.
PASCUALA: Why not?
LAURENCIA: When you see how I fight,
You won't need any Cid in armor bright!

                                        (*Exeunt omnes*)

SCENE 5

The Great Hall in the Commander's castle

*Frondoso stands with his hands tied in the presence
of the Commander, Flores, Ortuño and Cimbranos*

COMMANDER: Just hang him by the cord that dangles from
His wrists; in that way he will suffer more.
FRONDOSO: Oh, what a name your noble blood deserves!
COMMANDER: Now hang him from the nearest battlement.
FRONDOSO: I never did intend to kill you, sire.

                                    (*A commotion offstage*)

FLORES: Grande ruido suena.

COMENDADOR: ¿Ruido?

FLORES: Y de manera que interrumpen
tu justicia, señor.

ORTUÑO: Las puertas rompen.

COMENDADOR: ¡La puerta de mi casa, y siendo casa
de la encomienda!

FLORES: El pueblo junto viene.

ESCENA 6

Juan Rojo, dentro. Dichos; después, Mengo

JUAN ROJO (*dentro*): ¡Rompe, derriba, hunde, quema, abrasa!

ORTUÑO: Un popular motín mal se detiene.

COMENDADOR: ¡El pueblo contra mí!

FLORES: La furia pasa
tan adelante, que las puertas tiene
echadas por la tierra.

COMENDADOR: Desatadle.
Templa, Frondoso, ese villano alcalde.

FRONDOSO: Yo voy, señor; que amor les ha movido.

(*Vase*)

MENGO (*dentro*): ¡Vivan Fernando e Isabel, y mueran
los traidores!

FLORES: Señor, por Dios te pido
que no te hallen aquí.

COMENDADOR: Si perseveran,
este aposento es fuerte y defendido.
Ellos se volverán.

FLORES: Cuando se alteran
los pueblos agraviados, y resuelven,
nunca sin sangre o sin venganza vuelven.

COMENDADOR: En esta puerta, así como rastrillo,
su furor con las armas defendamos.

FRONDOSO (*dentro*): ¡Viva Fuenteovejuna!

FLORES: A loud noise sounds without.

COMMANDER: What noise is that?

FLORES: It comes at just this time and interrupts
  The execution of your rightful justice, sire.

ORTUÑO: They're breaking down the doors!

COMMANDER: The doors of my
  Headquarters of our Order broken down?

FLORES: They've come in force together from the town.

SCENE 6

Rojo's and Mengo's voices are heard outside

ROJO (*Offstage*):
  Now smash and burn the place, and kill them all!

ORTUÑO: The people in revolt are hard to check.

COMMANDER: The populace revolts against my rule?

FLORES: Their fury now has risen to the point
  That they have battered down your very doors.

COMMANDER: Untie him. Now, Frondoso, try to calm
  That peasant mayor.

FRONDOSO: I'll go, my lord, because
  Their love for me has moved them to attack.

(*Exit Frondoso*)

MENGO (*Offstage*): Long life to Ferdinand and Isabel,
  And death to traitors!

FLORES: Sire, I beg of you
  For Heaven's sake, don't let them find you here!

COMMANDER: They may persist, but this hall is quite strong;
  If we defend it well, they will retreat.

FLORES: Determined, outraged people—when they rise—
  Do not retreat without revenge in blood.

COMMANDER: At this great door, as if it were indeed
  An old portcullis, we shall take our stand
  And with our arms turn back this peasant band.

FRONDOSO (*Offstage*): Hurrah for Fuente Ovejuna!

COMENDADOR: ¡Qué caudillo!
Estoy por que a su furia acometamos.

FLORES: De la tuya, señor, me maravillo.

ESCENA 7

*Salen Esteban, Frondoso, Juan Rojo, Mengo, Barrildo
y labradores, todos armados. El Comendador,
Flores, Ortuño, Cimbranos*

ESTEBAN: Ya el tirano y los cómplices miramos.
¡Fuenteovejuna, los tiranos mueran!

COMENDADOR: Pueblo, esperad.

TODOS: Agravios nunca esperan.

COMENDADOR: Decídmelos a mí, que iré pagando
a fe de caballero esos errores.

TODOS: ¡Fuenteovejuna! ¡Viva el rey Fernando!
¡Mueran malos cristianos y traidores!

COMENDADOR: ¿No me queréis oír? Yo estoy hablando,
yo soy vuestro señor.

TODOS: Nuestros señores
son los Reyes Católicos.

COMENDADOR: Espera.

TODOS: ¡Fuenteovejuna, Fernán Gómez muera!

(*Pelean: el Comendador y los suyos vanse retirando y los
amotinados se entran persiguiéndolos*)

ESCENA 8

Salen las mujeres armadas; dichos, dentro

LAURENCIA: Parad en este puerto de esperanzas,
soldados atrevidos, no mujeres.

PASCUALA: ¿Los que mujeres son en las venganzas,
en él beban su sangre, es bien que esperes?

COMMANDER: What

A leader! Let us fight the fiery knave!

FLORES: I marvel, sire, that you can be so brave.

SCENE 7

Enter Esteban, Frondoso, Juan Rojo, Mengo,
Barrildo and other farmers, all armed

ESTEBAN: At last we face the tyrant and his gang!
  Now, Fuente Ovejuna, let them die!

COMMANDER: Just wait, my people . . .

ALL: Vengeance cannot wait.

COMMANDER: Now tell me your complaints; upon my word
  As I'm a noble, you shall have redress.

ALL: Hurrah for Fuente Ovejuna, and
  Long live our King Fernando! Hypocrites
  And traitors, die!

COMMANDER: Would you not hear me speak?
  I talk to you as your own rightful lord.

ALL: Our rightful rulers are the King and Queen!

COMMANDER: But wait!

ALL: Now, townsfolk, death to Don Fernán!

              (They fight. The Commander and his men leave
                    the stage, pursued by the insurgents)

SCENE 8

Enter Laurencia, Pascuala, Jacinta, and many other women,
  all armed. The men's voices are heard offstage

LAURENCIA: Wait here, right at this door. Remember that
  You are not women now, but soldiers bold.

PASCUALA: While men we thought were women take revenge
  And shed his blood, how can you tell us, "Wait"?

JACINTA: Su cuerpo recojamos en las lanzas.

PASCUALA: Todas son de esos mismos pareceres.

ESTEBAN (*dentro*): ¡Muere, traidor Comendador!

COMENDADOR (*dentro*): Ya muero.
  ¡Piedad, Señor, que en tu clemencia espero!

BARRILDO (*dentro*): Aquí está Flores.

MENGO (*dentro*): Dale a ese bellaco;
  que ése fué el que me dió dos mil azotes.

FRONDOSO (*dentro*): No me vengo si el alma no le saco.

LAURENCIA: No excusamos entrar.

PASCUALA: No te alborotes.
  Bien es guardar la puerta.

BARRILDO (*dentro*): ¡No me aplaco.
  Con lágrimas ahora, marquesotes!

LAURENCIA: Pascuala, yo entro dentro; que la espada
  no ha de estar tan sujeta ni envainada.

(*Vase*)

BARRILDO (*dentro*): Aquí está Ortuño.

FRONDOSO (*dentro*): Córtale la cara.

ESCENA 9

Sale Flores huyendo, y Mengo tras él

FLORES: ¡Mengo, piedad, que no soy yo el culpado!

MENGO: Cuando ser alcahuete no bastara,
  bastaba haberme el pícaro azotado.

PASCUALA: Dánoslo a las mujeres, Mengo, para . . .
  Acaba, por tu vida.

MENGO: Ya está dado;
  que no le quiero yo mayor castigo.

PASCUALA: Vengaré tus azotes.

MENGO: Eso digo.

JACINTA: ¡Ea, muera el traidor!

FLORES: ¡Entre mujeres!

JACINTA: Let us impale his body on our spears!

PASCUALA: We all are of one mind in this affair.

ESTEBAN (*Offstage*): Now die, you dog, Commander Don Fernán!

COMMANDER (*Offstage*):
I die . . . Have pity on my soul, oh God!

BARRILDO (*Offstage*): Here's Flores!

MENGO (*Offstage*):   Strike the swine! He is the one
Who laid two thousand lashes on my back.

FRONDOSO (*Offstage*): I shall not count myself avenged until
I've driven his black soul from out his corpse!

LAURENCIA: Let's enter now.

PASCUALA: Stand fast, and guard the door.

BARRILDO (*Offstage*): I'll not be softened now by all your tears,
You fops!

LAURENCIA: Pascuala, I must go inside;
I cannot keep my sword within its sheath.

(*Exit Laurencia*)

BARRILDO (*Offstage*): And here's Ortuño!

FRONDOSO (*Offstage*):   Slash his fiendish face!

SCENE 9

Enter Flores, pursued by Mengo

FLORES: Please, Mengo! Pity! I am not to blame.

MENGO: If being his procurer were not bad,
Your flogging me itself would merit death.

PASCUALA: Just hand him to us women, Mengo! Stop!

MENGO: I've had my fill of punishment. He's yours.

PASCUALA: I'll take full vengeance for your lashes now.

MENGO: Go right ahead!

JACINTA: Come on! Let's kill this rat!

FLORES: To die at women's hands?

JACINTA: ¿No le viene muy ancho?

PASCUALA: ¿Aqueso lloras?

JACINTA: Muere, concertador de sus placeres.

PASCUALA: ¡Ea, muera el traidor!

FLORES: ¡Piedad, señoras!

Sale Ortuño huyendo de Laurencia.

ORTUÑO: Mira que no soy yo . . .

LAURENCIA (*A las mujeres*): Ya sé quién eres.
   ¡Entrad, teñid las armas vencedoras
   en estos viles!

PASCUALA: Moriré matando.

TODAS: ¡Fuenteovejuna, y viva el rey Fernando!

(Vanse)

ESCENA 10

Habitación del Rey Don Fernando en Toro

Salen el Rey Don Fernando y Don Manrique, maestre

DON MANRIQUE: De modo la prevención
   fué, que el efecto esperado
   llegamos a ver logrado
   con poca contradicción.
   Hubo poca resistencia;
   y supuesto que la hubiera
   sin duda ninguna fuera
   de poca o ninguna esencia.
   Queda el de Cabra ocupado
   en conservación del puesto,
   por si volviere dispuesto
   a él el contrario osado.

JACINTA: Quite fitting, since
  You lived by pandering.

PASCUALA: It makes you weep?

JACINTA: Now die, procurer to his lechery!

PASCUALA: Yes, die, you dog!

FLORES: Have mercy, ladies, please!

Enter Ortuño, pursued by Laurencia.

ORTUÑO: Look, I am not the one you think I am . . .

LAURENCIA: I know full well just who you are, you swine!
  (*To the women*):
  Now enter! Bathe your swift, avenging swords
  In their vile blood!

PASCUALA: I'll conquer, or I'll die.

ALL: Hurrah for Fuente Ovejuna, and
  Long live our rightful lord, King Ferdinand!

(*Exeunt omnes*)

SCENE 10

King Ferdinand's palace in Toro

Enter the King and Don Manrique

MANRIQUE: Our preparations were so well devised
  That we gained our objective with small loss.
  Resistance was quite weak, but even if
  There had been some it would have been subdued.
  The Count of Cabra holds the town in case
  The enemy returns to the attack.

REY: Discreto el acuerdo fué,
   y que asista es conveniente,
   y reformando la gente,
   el paso tomado esté.
   Que con eso se asegura
   no podernos hacer mal
   Alfonso, que en Portugal
   tomar la fuerza procura.
   Y el de Cabra es bien que esté
   en ese sitio asistente,
   y como tan diligente,
   muestras de su valor dé;
   porque con esto asegura
   el daño que nos recela,
   y como fiel centinela
   el bien del reino procura.

ESCENA 11

Sale Flores, herido

FLORES: Católico rey Fernando,
   a quien el cielo concede
   la corona de Castilla,
   como a varón excelente:
   oye la mayor crueldad
   que se ha visto entre las gentes
   desde donde nace el sol
   hasta donde se obscurece.
REY: Repórtate.
FLORES: Rey supremo,
   mis heridas no consienten
   dilatar el triste caso,
   por ser mi vida tan breve.
   De Fuenteovejuna vengo,
   donde, con pecho inclemente,
   los vecinos de la villa
   a su señor dieron muerte.

KING: You have arranged things well between you two;
    His presence there is good. The next step now
    Is to regroup our forces and to thwart
    Alfonso, King of Portugal, who is
    Recruiting men so as to take the field.
    It's good to know that Ciudad Real
    Is held by Cabra, for we can depend
    On him to show his mettle in the fray;
    He thus can help to ward off any harm
    That threatens us, and as a sentinel
    The faithful Count will guard our kingdom well.

SCENE 11

Enter Flores, wounded

FLORES: Most Catholic King Ferdinand, on whom
    The crown of old Castile has been bestowed
    By God as the most worthy of all knights,
    Hear now the tale of foulest cruelty
    That ever has been seen in all the world,
    From where the sun comes up to where it sets.

KING: Contain yourself.
FLORES: My wounds, most sovereign King,
    Do not permit me to detail the case
    Because the life still left me is so short.
    I come from Fuente Ovejuna, where
    The village folk most ruthlessly have slain
    Their rightful lord, Commander Don Fernán.

Muerto Fernán Gómez queda
por sus súbditos aleves;
que vasallos indignados
con leve causa se atreven.
En título de tirano
le acumula todo el plebe,
y a la fuerza desta voz
el hecho fiero acometen;
y quebrantando su casa,
no atendiendo a que se ofrece
por la fe de caballero
a que pagará a quien debe,
no sólo no le escucharon,
pero con furia impaciente
rompen el cruzado pecho
con mil heridas crüeles,
y por las altas ventanas
le hacen que al suelo vuele,
adonde en picas y espadas
le recogen las mujeres.
Llévanle a una casa muerto
y a porfía, quien más puede
mesa su barba y cabello
y apriesa su rostro hieren.
En efecto fué la furia
tan grande que en ellos crece,
que las mayores tajadas
las orejas a ser vienen.
Sus armas borran con picas
y a voces dicen que quieren
tus reales armas fijar,
porque aquéllas les ofenden.
Saqueáronle la casa,
cual si de enemigos fuese,
y gozosos entre todos
han repartido sus bienes.
Lo dicho he visto escondido,
porque mi infelice suerte
en tal trance no permite
que mi vida se perdiese;
y así estuve todo el día
hasta que la noche viene,

This Gómez, murdered in a mutiny,
Lies victim to disloyal subjects there
Who dared attack him for some minor cause.
The epithet of "tyrant," hurled at him,
Inflamed the people to this heinous deed.
They broke into his castle, and despite
His offer—on his honor as a knight—
To recompense whoever had been harmed,
Not only did they fail to hear him out
But, restless in their wrath, they slashed his breast
(Which bore the red of Calatrava's Cross)
With countless cruel cuts. And then they hurled
Him from the topmost windows to the ground
Where women caught him on their swords and pikes.
They carried him—now dead—into a house
And fought among themselves to tear his hair,
To claw his beard, and then to hack his face:
Indeed their fury grew so great his ears
Were soon the largest pieces left intact.
With pikes they then ripped down his coat of arms
And shouted that they wished to raise instead
Your royal arms, because they hated his.
They sacked his castle next, as if it were
A foe's, and shared the loot among themselves.
I saw all this from where I lay concealed:
My ill-starred fate would not yet let me die.
And thus I spent the livelong day until

y salir pude escondido
para que cuenta te diese.
Haz, señor, pues eres justo
que la justa pena lleven
de tan riguroso caso
los bárbaros delincuentes:
mira que su sangre a voces
pide que tu rigor prueben.

REY: Estar puedes confiado
que sin castigo no queden.
El triste suceso ha sido
tal, que admirado me tiene,
y que vaya luego un juez
que lo averigüe conviene
y castigue los culpados
para ejemplo de las gentes.
Vaya un capitán con él,
porque seguridad lleve;
que tan grande atrevimiento
castigo ejemplar requiere;
y curad a ese soldado
de las heridas que tiene.

(*Vanse*)

ESCENA 12

Plaza en Fuenteovejuna

*Salen los labradores y las labradoras, con la
cabeza de Fernán Gómez en una lanza; músicos*

MÚSICOS (*Cantan*): *¡Muchos años vivan
Isabel y Fernando,
y mueran los tiranos!*

BARRILDO: Diga su copla Frondoso.

Night fell, when I was able to escape
And come to give you my report of this.
My liege, as you are just, take just redress
For this foul crime; his noble blood demands
Revenge for being shed by peasant hands.

KING: Be reassured that they shall not remain
   Unpunished. I am so amazed at this
Sad tale that I shall send a judge at once
To look into the case and punish those
Found guilty; sheer rebellion such as this
Deserves a punishment severe enough
To serve as an example to the rest.
The judge shall not lack for security:
A captain shall go with him, have no fear.
Now bind the wounds of this poor soldier here.

(Exeunt omnes)

SCENE 12

The Town Square in Fuente Ovejuna

*Enter Esteban, Frondoso, Barrildo, Mengo, Laurencia, Pascuala,
councilmen, farmers and their womenfolk, bearing the head
of Commander Don Fernán on a pike. Musicians
accompany them*

MUSICIANS (*Singing*): Long life to Isabel and Ferdinand,
                And death to all the tyrants in the land!

BARRILDO: Come now, Frondoso, let us hear your verse.

FRONDOSO: Ya va mi copla, a la fe;
  si le faltare algún pie,
  enmiéndelo el más curioso.
  "¡Vivan la bella Isabel,
  y Fernando de Aragón,
  pues que para en uno son,
  él con ella, ella con él!
  A los cielos San Miguel
  lleve a los dos de las manos.
  ¡Vivan muchos años,
  y mueran los tiranos!"

LAURENCIA: Diga Barrildo.

BARRILDO: Ya va;
  que a fe que la he pensado.

PASCUALA: Si la dices con cuidado,
  buena y rebuena será.

BARRILDO: "¡Vivan los reyes famosos
  muchos años, pues que tienen
  la victoria, y a ser vienen
  nuestros dueños venturosos!
  Salgan siempre victoriosos
  de gigantes y de enanos
  y ¡mueran los tiranos!"

MÚSICOS (*Cantan*): *¡Muchos años vivan*
  Isabel y Fernando,
  y mueran los tiranos!

LAURENCIA: Diga Mengo.

FRONDOSO: Mengo diga.

MENGO: Yo soy poeta donado.

PASCUALA: Mejor dirás lastimado
  el envés[1] de la barriga.

MENGO: "Una mañana en domingo
  me mandó azotar aquél,
  de manera que el rabel
  daba espantoso respingo;
  pero ahora que los pringo
  ¡vivan los reyes cristánigos,
  y mueran los tiránigos!"

[1] *envés* revés

FRONDOSO: Here comes my poem now, upon my faith!
  If purists find the meter wrong in parts,
  It may be changed to please their little hearts.
           Long live Queen Isabel
           And good King Ferdinand!
           As loving man and wife
           May they rule o'er this land.
           When their work here is done
           St. Michael's angel band
           Will waft them up above
           To Heaven hand in hand.
           Long life to them, and death
           To tyrants in our land!

LAURENCIA: Barrildo's turn comes next.

BARRILDO: Well, here it is.
  Lord knows I've given it a lot of thought.

PASCUALA: Then do it justice: please recite it well;
  It must be good—but only time can tell.

BARRILDO: Long live our famous King and Queen!
           They've won the victory;
       They are our royal sovereigns,
           May they live happily.
      May victory be always theirs
           O'er troubles great and small;
      And as for tyrants in our land,
           May death come take them all!

MUSICIANS (*Singing*): Long life to Isabel and Ferdinand,
           And death to all the tyrants in the land!

LAURENCIA: And now for Mengo.

FRONDOSO: Yes, it's Mengo's turn.

MENGO: You know, I'm quite a gifted poet, too.

PASCUALA: You mean a beaten poet! We know where
  You got a gift—upon your *derrière!*

MENGO: He ordered them to tan my hide
           One Sunday morning bright;
       They flogged me on my poor backside,
           It gave me quite a fright.
      But now my side has gotten back,
           And they'll be no more seen;
      May tyrants die upon the rack:
           Long live our King and Queen!

MÚSICOS: *¡Vivan muchos años!*, etc. . . .

ESTEBAN: Quita la cabeza allá.

MENGO: Cara tiene de ahorcado.

REGIDOR: Ya las armas han llegado.

ESCENA 13

Saca un escudo Juan Rojo con las armas reales

ESTEBAN: Mostrá [2] las armas acá.

JUAN ROJO: ¿Adónde se han de poner?

REGIDOR: Aquí, en el Ayuntamiento.

ESTEBAN: ¡Bravo escudo!

BARRILDO: ¡Qué contento!

FRONDOSO: Ya comienza a amanecer,
con este sol, nuestro día.

ESTEBAN: ¡Vivan Castilla y León,
y las barras de Aragón,
y muera la tiranía!
Advertid, Fuenteovejuna,
a las palabras de un viejo;
que el admitir su consejo
no ha dañado vez ninguna.

FRONDOSO: ¿Qué es tu consejo?

ESTEBAN: Morir
diciendo *Fuenteovejuna*,
y a nadie saquen de aquí.

FRONDOSO: Es el camino derecho.
Fuenteovejuna lo ha hecho.

ESTEBAN: ¿Queréis responder así?

TODOS: Sí.

ESTEBAN: Ahora pues, yo quiero ser
ahora el pesquisidor,
para ensayarnos mejor
en lo que habemos de hacer.
Sea Mengo el que esté puesto
en el tormento.

[2] *mostrá*   mostrad

MUSICIANS (*Singing*): Long life to Isabel and Ferdinand,
And death to all the tyrants in the land!

ESTEBAN: Now take his horrid head down off that pike.

MENGO: His face looks just as though he had been hanged.

COUNCILMAN: Here comes the scutcheon with the royal arms.

SCENE 13

*Enter Juan Rojo, bringing a shield which
displays the royal coat of arms*

ESTEBAN: Hold up the royal arms, so we can see.

ROJO: Where shall we place them?

COUNCILMAN: Put them right up here
Upon our own Town Hall.

ESTEBAN: A noble shield!

BARRILDO: What joy!

FRONDOSO: This shield is like the rising sun:
It means a bright new day for everyone.

ESTEBAN: Long live Castile, León, and Aragón,
And death to tyranny! Now hear my words,
Oh Fuente Ovejuna: the advice
Of this old man has never brought you harm.

FRONDOSO: And what is your advice?

ESTEBAN: That each of you
Say "Fuente Ovejuna" if they ask
Who did it—even if you die for it.

FRONDOSO: Well, that's the truth: the guilty one indeed
Is Fuente Ovejuna—all of us!

ESTEBAN: You all agree to answer just like that?

ALL: Yes, yes!

ESTEBAN: Now I'll pretend I am the judge,
So we can practice what we are to do.
Let Mengo be the one who's on the rack.

MENGO: ¿No hallaste
otro más flaco?

ESTEBAN: ¿Pensaste
que era de veras?

MENGO: Di presto.

ESTEBAN: ¿Quién mató al Comendador?

MENGO: Fuenteovejuna lo hizo.

ESTEBAN: Perro, ¿si te martirizo?

MENGO: Aunque me matéis, señor.

ESTEBAN: Confiesa, ladrón.

MENGO: Confieso.

ESTEBAN: Pues ¿quién fué?

MENGO: Fuenteovejuna.

ESTEBAN: Dadle otra vuelta.

MENGO: Es ninguna.

ESTEBAN: Cagajón[1] para el proceso.

ESCENA 14

Sale el otro Regidor

REGIDOR: ¿Qué hacéis desta suerte aquí?

FRONDOSO: ¿Qué ha sucedido, Cuadrado?

REGIDOR: Pesquisidor ha llegado.

ESTEBAN: Echá[2] todos por ahí.

REGIDOR: Con él viene un capitán.

ESTEBAN: Venga el diablo: ya sabéis
lo que responder tenéis.

REGIDOR: El pueblo prendiendo van,
sin dejar alma ninguna.

[1] *cagajón*   estiércol

[2] *echá*   echad

MENGO: You couldn't find a thinner one to stretch?

ESTEBAN: You thought we really meant to do it, eh?

MENGO: Begin!

ESTEBAN: "Who killed Commander Don Fernán?"

MENGO: "Sir, Fuente Ovejuna did the deed."

ESTEBAN: "You dog! I'll have you broken on the rack!"

MENGO: "It's true, although I die for it, my lord!"

ESTEBAN: "Confess, you rogue!"

MENGO: "Yes, yes! I shall confess!"

ESTEBAN: "Well, tell me, then: who is the guilty one?"

MENGO: "It's Fuente Ovejuna."

ESTEBAN: "Give the screws
     Another turn."

MENGO: "Go right ahead; I'm bold!"

ESTEBAN: A fig for any trial they care to hold!

SCENE 14

Enter the other Councilman

COUNCILMAN: What are you all engaged in here, my friends?

FRONDOSO: Why, what's the matter, friend Cuadrado, now?

COUNCILMAN: A judge has come.

ESTEBAN: Then scatter to your homes.

COUNCILMAN: A captain and some troops are with him, too.

ESTEBAN: Although the Devil came, we would not care!
     You all know what your answer is to be.

COUNCILMAN: They are arresting everyone on sight,
     With no exceptions.

ESTEBAN: Que no hay que tener temor.
   ¿Quién mató al Comendador,
   Mengo?

MENGO: ¿Quién? Fuenteovejuna.

(Vanse)

ESCENA 15

Habitación del Maestre de Calatrava en Almagro

Salen el Maestre y un Soldado

MAESTRE: ¡Qué tal caso ha sucedido!
   Infelice fué su suerte.
   Estoy por darte la muerte
   por la nueva que has traído.

SOLDADO: Yo, señor, soy mensajero,
   y enojarte no es mi intento.

MAESTRE: ¡Que a tal tuvo atrevimiento
   un pueblo enojado y fiero!
   Iré con quinientos hombres
   y la villa he de asolar;
   en ella no ha de quedar
   ni aun memoria de los nombres.

SOLDADO: Señor, tu enojo reporta;
   porque ellos al rey se han dado,
   y no tener enojado
   al rey es lo que te importa.

MAESTRE: ¿Cómo al rey se pueden dar,
   si de la encomienda son?

SOLDADO: Con él sobre esa razón
   podrás luego pleitear.

MAESTRE: Por pleito ¿cuándo salió
   lo que él le entregó en sus manos?
   Son señores soberanos,
   y tal reconozco yo.

ESTEBAN: There's no need to fear.
Now, Mengo, tell me: who killed Don Fernán?

MENGO: Who was it? Fuente Ovejuna, sir!

SCENE 15

Home of the Master of Calatrava in Almagro

Enter the Master, and a soldier

MASTER: To think that such a thing could happen there!
How sad a fate! I feel like putting you
To death for bringing me such news as this.

SOLDIER: I come as just a simple messenger;
To anger you was not my purpose, sire.

MASTER: To think the townsfolk were so roused that they
Could dare commit a vicious crime like that!
I'll take five hundred soldiers and destroy
The town; no one shall even recollect
The names of men who once lived in that place.

SOLDIER: Contain your anger, sire; they have declared
Their loyalty to King Fernando's cause.
It would be best that you not anger him.

MASTER: How can they give allegiance to the King?
The village is a part of our estates.

SOLDIER: Your Order's legal claims can be discussed
With King Fernando later, sire.

MASTER: Since when
Does he relinquish anything that falls
Into his hands? I have no case at law:
The King and Queen are sovereign, that I know.

Por saber que al rey se han dado
me reportará mi enojo,
y ver su presencia escojo
por lo más bien acertado;
que puesto que tenga culpa
en casos de gravedad,
en todo mi poca edad
viene a ser quien me disculpa.
Con vergüenza voy; mas es
honor quien puede obligarme,
e importa no descuidarme
en tan honrado interés.

(*Vanse*)

ESCENA 16

Plaza de Fuenteovejuna

Sale Laurencia sola

LAURENCIA: Amando, recelar daño en lo amado
nueva pena de amor se considera;
que quien en lo que ama daño espera
aumenta en el temor nuevo cuidado.
El firme pensamiento desvelado,
si le aflige el temor, fácil se altera;
que no es a firme fe pena ligera
ver llevar el temor el bien robado.
Mi esposo adoro; la ocasión que veo
al temor de su daño me condena,
si no le ayuda la felice suerte.
Al bien suyo se inclina mi deseo:
si está presente, está cierta mi pena;
si está en ausencia, está cierta mi muerte.

Since you have told me that the town has placed
Itself in royal hands, I'll curb my wrath;
It's best to seek an audience with him.
For though he may declare I am to blame,
My very youth will be my best defense.
My honor calls me, yet I go with shame;
For honor's sake I must not take offense.

(Exeunt)

SCENE 16

The Town Square in Fuente Ovejuna

Enter Laurencia, alone

LAURENCIA: The fear that harm may come to one you love
Is rightly thought of as a double fear;
New dread is born with warnings from above:
A lover senses when some harm is near.
A firm and steadfast mind, if fear but start,
Is quickly undermined by pain and woe;
And grief can oft afflict the stoutest heart
If one adored is captured by the foe.
I love my husband, and the lot I see
In store for him condemns me to new fears,
Unless some happy turn of fate for me
Can keep him safe in answer to my tears.
With him in town, a price is on his head;
With him away, I would as lief be dead!

ESCENA 17

Sale Frondoso

FRONDOSO: ¡Mi Laurencia!

LAURENCIA: ¡Esposo amado!
 ¿Cómo a estar aquí te atreves?

FRONDOSO: ¿Esas resistencias debes
 a mi amoroso cuidado?

LAURENCIA: Mi bien, procura guardarte,
 porque tu daño recelo.

FRONDOSO: No quiera, Laurencia, el cielo
 que tal llegue a disgustarte.

LAURENCIA: ¿No temes ver el rigor
 que por los demás sucede,
 y el furor con que procede
 aqueste pesquisidor?
 Procura guardar la vida.
 Huye, tu daño no esperes.

FRONDOSO: ¿Cómo que procure quieres
 cosa tan mal recibida?
 ¿Es bien que los demás deje
 en el peligro presente
 y de tu vista me ausente?
 No me mandes que me aleje;
 porque no es puesto en razón
 que por evitar mi daño,
 sea con mi sangre extraño
 en tan terrible ocasión.

(Voces dentro)

 Voces parece que he oído,
 y son si yo mal no siento,
 de alguno que dan tormento.
 Oye con atento oído.

SCENE 17

Enter Frondoso

FRONDOSO: Laurencia, dear!

LAURENCIA: Belovèd husband mine!
How is it that you dare to be here now?

FRONDOSO: Is that the way to greet my loving care?

LAURENCIA: My love, I fear for you; be careful, dear.

FRONDOSO: I hope to Heaven that my coming here
Does not displease you . . .

LAURENCIA: Are you not afraid
When you can see how harshly that stern judge
Proceeds against the others? Save your life!
Be off, and do not wait for harm to strike.

FRONDOSO: Why try to save a life so ill-received?
And is it right to leave the others now
In such great peril, and to leave you, too?
Please do not tell me I should go away,
For it is inconceivable that I
Should now desert my kin at such a time
To save myself.

(Voices are heard offstage)

I seem to hear a cry;
Unless I am mistaken, what I hear
Is someone being tortured. Lend an ear . . .

ESCENA 18

Un Juez, Esteban, un niño, Pascuala y Mengo,
en la cárcel inmediata; dichos

JUEZ (*dentro*): Decid la verdad, buen viejo.

FRONDOSO: Un viejo, Laurencia mía,
atormentan.

LAURENCIA: ¡Qué porfía!

ESTEBAN (*dentro*): Déjenme un poco.

JUEZ (*dentro*): Ya os dejo.
Decid: ¿quién mató a Fernando?

ESTEBAN (*dentro*): Fuenteovejuna lo hizo.

LAURENCIA: Tu nombre, padre, eternizo.

FRONDOSO: ¡Bravo caso!

JUEZ (*dentro*): Ese muchacho
aprieta. Perro, yo sé
que lo sabes. Di quién fué.
¿Callas? Aprieta, borracho.

NIÑO (*dentro*): Fuenteovejuna, señor.

JUEZ (*dentro*): ¡Por vida del rey, villanos,
que os ahorque con mis manos!
¿Quién mató al Comendador?

FRONDOSO: ¡Qué a un niño le den tormento
y niegue de aquesta suerte!

LAURENCIA: ¡Bravo pueblo!

FRONDOSO: Bravo y fuerte.

JUEZ (*dentro*): Esa mujer al momento
en ese potro tened.
Dale esa mancuerda luego.

LAURENCIA: Ya está de cólera ciego.

JUEZ (*dentro*): Que os he de matar, creed,
en este potro, villanos.
¿Quién mató al Comendador?

PASCUALA (*dentro*): Fuenteovejuna, señor.

JUEZ (*dentro*): ¡Dale!

FRONDOSO: Pensamientos vanos.

LAURENCIA: Pascuala niega, Frondoso.

SCENE 18

The voices of the Judge, Esteban, a boy, Pascuala and
Mengo are heard from the jail, which is glimpsed
at the edge of the stage

JUDGE (*Offstage*): Now tell the truth, old man.

FRONDOSO: They're torturing
Some poor old man, Laurencia.

LAURENCIA: What a shame!

ESTEBAN (*Offstage*): Let loose a little.

JUDGE (*Offstage*): Good! Relax those screws!
All right, then; tell me. Who killed Don Fernán?

ESTEBAN (*Offstage*): 'Twas Fuente Ovejuna did it, sir.

LAURENCIA: I praise your name forever, father dear.

FRONDOSO: He kept his word.

JUDGE (*Offstage*): Now seize that little boy.
You whelp, I'm sure you know. Now tell me who
It was . . . So silent? Tighten up those screws!

BOY (*Offstage*): 'Twas Fuente Ovejuna did it, sir.

JUDGE (*Offstage*): Upon the King's own life, you peasant dogs,
I'll hang you with my own judicial hands!
Who was it here that murdered Don Fernán?

FRONDOSO: To think that they could rack a little child
That way, and he refuse to tell!

LAURENCIA: Brave folk!

FRONDOSO: Yes, brave and steadfast.·

JUDGE (*Offstage*): Seize that woman there,
And place her on the rack. Now, tighten up!

LAURENCIA: He's blind with rage.

JUDGE (*Offstage*): Believe me, I shall kill
You all upon the rack, you peasant swine,
Unless you tell me who killed Don Fernán!

PASCUALA (*Offstage*): 'Twas Fuente Ovejuna did it, sir.

JUDGE (*Offstage, to torturer*): Now, twist!

FRONDOSO: In vain.

LAURENCIA: Pascuala's holding out!

FRONDOSO: Niegan niños: ¿qué te espantas?

JUEZ (*dentro*): Parece que los encantas.
  ¡Aprieta!

PASCUALA (*dentro*): ¡Ay cielo piadoso!

JUEZ (*dentro*): ¡Aprieta, infame! ¿Estás sordo?

PASCUALA (*dentro*): Fuenteovejuna lo hizo.

JUEZ (*dentro*): Traedme aquel más rollizo,
  ese desnudo, ese gordo.

LAURENCIA: ¡Pobre Mengo! El es sin duda.

FRONDOSO: Temo que ha de confesar.

MENGO (*dentro*): ¡Ay, ay!

JUEZ (*dentro*): Comienza a apretar.

MENGO (*dentro*): ¡Ay!

JUEZ (*dentro*): ¿Es menester ayuda?

MENGO (*dentro*): ¡Ay, ay!

JUEZ (*dentro*): ¿Quién mató, villano,
  al señor Comendador?

MENGO (*dentro*): ¡Ay, yo lo diré, señor!

JUEZ (*dentro*): Afloja un poco la mano.

FRONDOSO: El confiesa.

JUEZ (*dentro*): Al palo aplica
  la espalda.

MENGO (*dentro*): Quedo; que yo
  lo diré.

JUEZ (*dentro*): ¿Quién lo mató?

MENGO (*dentro*): Señor, Fuenteovejunica.

JUEZ (*dentro*): ¿Hay tan gran bellaquería?
  Del dolor se están burlando.
  En quien estaba esperando,
  niega con mayor porfía.
  Dejadlos; que estoy cansado.

FRONDOSO: ¡Oh, Mengo, bien te haga Dios!
  Temor que tuve de dos,
  el tuyo me lo ha quitado.

FRONDOSO: If boys hold out, why are you so amazed?

JUDGE (*Offstage, to torturer*):
  Twist harder! You just tickle them, it seems.

PASCUALA (*Offstage*): Oh, God!

JUDGE (*Offstage, to torturer*):
              Twist hard, you scoundrel! Are you deaf?

PASCUALA (*Offstage*): 'Twas Fuente Ovejuna did it, sir.

JUDGE (*Offstage*): Now bring me that half-naked fatty there.

LAURENCIA: Poor Mengo! It is he, without a doubt.

FRONDOSO: I fear he may break down and talk.

MENGO (*Offstage*):   Oh! Oh!

JUDGE (*Offstage, to torturer*):
  Get on with it! Now turn that lever!

MENGO (*Offstage*):   Oh!

JUDGE (*Offstage, to torturer*): Do you need help?

MENGO (*Offstage*):   Oh! Oh!

JUDGE (*Offstage*):   You peasant knave,
  Who was it here that murdered Don Fernán?

MENGO (*Offstage*): I'll tell you, sir.

JUDGE (*Offstage, to torturer*):   Relax it just a bit.

FRONDOSO: He is confessing.

JUDGE (*Offstage, to torturer*): Lean against that rod!

MENGO (*Offstage*): Oh! Oh! I've had enough. I'll tell you, sir.

JUDGE (*Offstage*): Who killed him, then?

MENGO (*Offstage*):   My lord, it was our good
  Old Fuente Ovejuna did the deed.

JUDGE (*Offstage*): I've never seen such trickery! They seem
  To laugh at agony. The one from whom
  I hoped for most, resists most stubbornly.
  Just let them go; I am exhausted now.

FRONDOSO: God bless you, Mengo. I was trembling here,
  But you've shown strength for two, and banished fear.

ESCENA 19

Salen Mengo, Barrildo y el Regidor

BARRILDO: ¡Vítor, Mengo!

REGIDOR: Y con razón.

BARRILDO: ¡Mengo, vítor!

FRONDOSO: Eso digo.

MENGO: ¡Ay, ay!

BARRILDO: Toma, come, bebe, amigo.

MENGO: ¡Ay, ay! ¿Qué es?

BARRILDO: Diacitrón.

MENGO: ¡Ay, ay!

FRONDOSO: Echa de beber.

BARRILDO: Ya va.

FRONDOSO: Bien lo cuela. Bueno está.

LAURENCIA: Dale otra vez a comer.

MENGO: ¡Ay, ay!

BARRILDO: Esta va por mí.

LAURENCIA: Solemnemente lo embebe.

FRONDOSO: El que bien niega bien bebe.

REGIDOR: ¿Quieres otra?

MENGO: ¡Ay, ay! Sí, sí.

FRONDOSO: Bebe; que bien lo mereces.

LAURENCIA: A vez por vuelta las cuela.

FRONDOSO: Arrópale, que se hiela.

BARRILDO: ¿Quieres más?

MENGO: Sí, otras tres veces.
    ¡Ay, ay!

FRONDOSO: Si hay vino pregunta.

BARRILDO: Sí hay; bebe a tu placer,
    que quien niega ha de beber.
    ¿Qué tiene?

MENGO: Una cierta punta.
    Vamos; que me arromadizo.

SCENE 19

Barrildo and the Councilman come out of the jail with Mengo

BARRILDO: Hurrah for Mengo!

COUNCILMAN: Absolutely right!

BARRILDO: Hurrah for Mengo!

FRONDOSO: That's what I say, too.

MENGO: Oh, oh, my aching back!

BARRILDO: Come drink and eat.

MENGO: Oh, oh! What is this stuff?

BARRILDO: Sweet lemon peel.

MENGO: Oh, oh!

FRONDOSO: Pour him a drink.

BARRILDO: Yes, here it comes.

FRONDOSO: It's real good stuff: it gurgles down his throat.

LAURENCIA: Now food again.

MENGO: Ah!

BARRILDO: This drink is on me.

LAURENCIA: Just look how solemnly he drinks his wine.

FRONDOSO: A man who laughs at racks has earned the right
To be a serious drinker if he likes.

COUNCILMAN: Now how about another?

MENGO: Yes, indeed!

LAURENCIA: One drink for every turn upon the rack.

FRONDOSO: Now cover him; he has a chill.

BARRILDO (*To Mengo*): Some wine?

MENGO: Yes, three more rounds. Oh, oh!

FRONDOSO: He asks for wine.

BARRILDO: There's lots of it: drink to your heart's content,
For one who stands the rack should drink his fill.
What's wrong?

MENGO: This wine is just a little sharp.
And I am catching cold.

FRONDOSO: Es aloque[1]: éste es mejor.
  ¿Quién mató al Comendador?
MENGO: Fuenteovejunica lo hizo.

                         (*Vanse*)

ESCENA 20

FRONDOSO: Justo es que honores le den.
  Pero decidme, mi amor,
  ¿quién mató al Comendador?
LAURENCIA: Fuenteovejuna, mi bien.
FRONDOSO: ¿Quién le mató?
LAURÉNCIA: Dasme espanto.
  Pues Fuenteovejuna fué.
FRONDOSO: Y yo ¿con qué te maté?
LAURENCIA: ¿Con qué? Con quererme tanto.

                         (*Vanse*)

ESCENA 21

Habitación de los Reyes en Tordesillas

Salen el Rey y la Reina y Don Manrique

DOÑA ISABEL: No entendí, señor, hallaros
  aquí, y es buena mi suerte.
REY: En nueva gloria convierte
  mi vista el bien de miraros.
  Iba a Portugal de paso
  y llegar aquí fué fuerza.
DOÑA ISABEL: Vuestra majestad le tuerza,
  siendo conveniente el caso.
REY: ¿Cómo dejáis a Castilla?
DOÑA ISABEL: En paz queda, quieta y llana.
REY: Siendo vos la que la allana,
  no lo tengo a maravilla.

   [1] *aloque*   vino blanco y tinto

FRONDOSO: Here, try this wine;
  It's better. Tell me, who killed Don Fernán?
MENGO: 'Twas Fuente Ovejuna did it, sir!

                    (*Exeunt all but Frondoso and Laurencia*)

SCENE 20

FRONDOSO: It is but right that Mengo should be praised.
  But tell me, love: Who did kill Don Fernán?

LAURENCIA: 'Twas Fuente Ovejuna did it, dear.
FRONDOSO: Now, just between us two, who really did?
LAURENCIA: You frighten me! I've told you clearly, love:
  'Twas Fuente Ovejuna did it, dear.
FRONDOSO: And I? Just how did I slay you, my dear?
LAURENCIA: By making me love you so much, it's clear!

                                        (*Exeunt*)

SCENE 21

The Royal Palace in Tordesillas

*Enter the King, Queen, and Don Manrique,
Master of Santiago*

ISABEL: I did not know that I would see you here,
  My lord; thus I am fortunate indeed.
KING: My eyes behold new glory, seeing you;
  En route to Portugal, I had to stop.

ISABEL: I'm happy that Your Majesty has found
  It good to change his route, and wants to stop.
KING: And how were things when you left Old Castile?
ISABEL: All quiet and serene, Your Majesty.
KING: Since you have calmed it, I am not surprised.

DON MANRIQUE: Para ver vuestra presencia
el maestre de Calatrava,
que aquí de llegar acaba,
pide que le deis licencia.

DOÑA ISABEL: Verle tenía deseado.

DON MANRIQUE: Mi fe, señora, os empeño;
que, aunque es en edad pequeño,
es valeroso soldado.

(Vase)

ESCENA 22

Sale el Maestre

MAESTRE: Rodrigo Téllez Girón,
que de loaros no acaba,
maestre de Calatrava,
os pide humilde perdón.
Confieso que fuí engañado,
y que excedí de lo justo
en cosas de vuestro gusto,
como mal aconsejado.
El consejo de Fernando
y el interés me engañó;
injusto fué; y así, yo
perdón humilde os demando.
Y si recibir merezco
esta merced que suplico,
desde aquí me certifico
en que a serviros me ofrezco,
y que en aquesta jornada
de Granada, adonde vais,
os prometo que veáis,
el valor que hay en mi espada;
donde sacándola apenas,
dándoles fieras congojas,
plantaré mis cruces rojas
sobre sus altas almenas;
y más quinientos soldados
en serviros emplearé,
junto con la firma y fe
de en mi vida disgustaros.

MANRIQUE: Now Calatrava's Master has arrived,
Your Majesties, and begs an audience.

ISABEL: It long has been my wish to see that youth.
MANRIQUE: I urge that you do so, Your Majesty;
Though young in years, he is a valiant man.

(*Exit Manrique*)

SCENE 22

Enter Don Rodrigo, Master of the Order of Calatrava

RODRIGO: Rodrigo Téllez, Master of the Cross
Of Calatrava, who will never cease
To praise Your Majesties, most humbly begs
Forgiveness. I confess that, ill-advised,
I did exceed the bounds of what was right
In matters dear to both Your Majesties.
Deceived by Don Fernán's false counselling,
I let self-interest lead me astray.
All this was wrong. I therefore humbly plead
For pardon. If I merit this great boon
I pledge in faith to serve Your Majesties
Against Granada in the next campaign.
I promise you that when I draw my sword
The Moors shall suffer sorely; you will see
Me plant the red of Calatrava's Cross
Upon their topmost battlements, for my
Five hundred men will all be serving you.
And I shall sign, upon my faith, an oath
That never more will I displease you both.

REY: Alzad, maestre, del suelo;
   que siempre que hayáis venido,
   seréis muy bien recibido.

MAESTRE: Sois de afligidos consuelo.

DOÑA ISABEL: Vos con valor peregrino
   sabéis bien decir y hacer.

MAESTRE: Vos sois una bella Ester
   y vos un Jerjes divino.

ESCENA 23

Sale don Manrique

DON MANRIQUE: Señor, el pesquisidor
   que a Fuenteovejuna ha ido
   con el despacho ha venido
   a verse ante tu valor.

REY (*a la Reina*): Sed juez destos agresores.

MAESTRE: Si a vos, señor, no mirara,
   sin duda les enseñara
   a matar comendadores.

REY (*al Maestre*): Eso ya no os toca a vos.

DOÑA ISABEL: Yo confieso que he de ver
   el cargo en vuestro poder,
   si me lo concede Dios.

ESCENA 24

Sale el Juez

JUEZ: A Fuenteovejuna fuí
   de la suerte que has mandado
   y con especial cuidado
   y diligencia asistí.
   Haciendo averiguación
   del cometido delito,
   una hoja no se ha escrito
   que sea en comprobación;

KING: Rise up, good Don Rodrigo, from your knees.
  Since you have come here of your own free will,
  Your explanation will be well received.

RODRIGO: You are the comfort of the sorrowful.

ISABEL: And you, a valiant knight who can combine
  Outstanding deeds with very gallant words.

RODRIGO: You are the lovely Esther of our day;
  And you, sire, Xerxes, splendid in array.

SCENE 23

Don Manrique re-enters

MANRIQUE: Your Majesty, the judge that you dispatched
  To Fuente Ovejuna has returned,
  And would present his full report to you.

KING (*To Queen*): Now you shall judge these lawless rioters.

RODRIGO: Were I not in your royal presence, sire,
  I'd teach base peasants not to kill their lords!

KING: Young Master, this is now not your affair.

ISABEL: Before God, I confess I'd rather see
  Your Majesty take charge of this for me.

SCENE 24

The Judge enters

JUDGE: I went to Fuente Ovejuna, sire,
  As you commanded me. With diligence
  And special care I looked into the crime
  Committed, but I have not written down
  A single page of evidence as proof.

porque conformes a una,
con un valeroso pecho,
en pidiendo quién lo ha hecho,
responden: "Fuenteovejuna".
Trescientos he atormentado
con no pequeño rigor,
y te prometo, señor,
que más que esto no he sacado.
Hasta niños de diez años
al potro arrimé, y no ha sido
posible haberlo inquirido
ni por halagos ni engaños.
Y pues tan mal se acomoda
el poderlo averiguar,
o los has de perdonar,
o matar la villa toda.
Todos vienen ante ti
para más certificarte:
dellos podrás informarte.

REY: Que entren, pues vienen, les di.

ESCENA 25

Esteban, Alonso, Frondoso, Laurencia, Mengo
Labradores y labradoras

LAURENCIA (*Aparte*): ¿Aquestos los reyes son?

FRONDOSO (*Aparte*): Y en Castilla poderosos.

LAURENCIA (*Aparte*): Por mi fe, que son hermosos:
   ¡bendígalos San Antón!

DOÑA ISABEL: ¿Los agresores son éstos?

ESTEBAN: Fuenteovejuna, señora,
   que humildes llegan ahora
   para serviros dispuestos.
   La sobrada tiranía
   y el insufrible rigor
   del muerto Comendador,
   que mil insultos hacía,
   fué el autor de tanto daño.
   Las haciendas nos robaba
   y las doncellas forzaba,
   siendo de piedad extraño.

This is because they all (I must confess
They were courageous) answered as one man,
When questioned as to who killed Don Fernán,
" 'Twas Fuente Ovejuna did it, sir."
I put three hundred harshly on the rack
And yet, Your Majesty, I could extract
No further word from any one of them.
I even put small boys ten years of age
Upon the rack: it was impossible
To learn a word despite all promises
And cunning tricks. Since I did not succeed
In finding out, I must suggest that you
Should either pardon them, Your Majesty,
Or execute the village to a man.
They all have come along as further proof
Of what I say, and wish to testify.

KING: Since they have come, then let them in, say I.

SCENE 25

Enter Esteban, Alonso, Frondoso, Laurencia,
Mengo, and the other villagers

LAURENCIA (*Aside*): Are they the King and Queen?
FRONDOSO (*Aside*):   They are indeed,
  And they hold sway in Old and New Castile.
LAURENCIA (*Aside*): Upon my faith, they are a handsome pair;
  May they be blessed by good Saint Anthony!
ISABEL: Are these the people charged with the attack?
ESTEBAN: The town of Fuente Ovejuna stands
  Before Your Majesty, and humbly begs
  To be of service. The late Don Fernán,
  Who ruled with overbearing tyranny
  And cruel despotism, was the cause
  Of all this, with a thousand vile affronts.
  He robbed our farms and raped our village girls:
  He was a pitilessly evil man . . .

FRONDOSO: Tanto, que aquesta zagala,
 que el cielo me ha concedido,
 en que tan dichoso he sido
 que nadie en dicha me iguala,
 cuando conmigo casó,
 aquella noche primera,
 mejor que si suya fuera,
 a su casa la llevó;
 y a no saberse guardar
 ella, que en virtud florece,
 ya manifiesto parece
 lo que pudiera pasar.

MENGO: ¿No es ya tiempo que hable yo?
 Si me dais licencia, entiendo
 que os admiraréis, sabiendo
 del modo que me trató.
 Porque quise defender
 una moza de su gente,
 que con término insolente
 fuerza la querían hacer,
 aquel perverso Nerón
 de manera me ha tratado,
 que el reverso me ha dejado
 como rueda de salmón.
 Tocaron mis atabales
 tres hombres con tal porfía,
 que aun pienso que todavía
 me duran los cardenales.
 Gasté en este mal prolijo,
 porque el cuero se me curta,
 polvos de arrayán y murta
 más que vale mi cortijo.

ESTEBAN: Señor, tuyos ser queremos.
 Rey nuestro eres natural,
 y con título de tal
 ya tus armas puesto habemos.
 Esperamos tu clemencia
 y que veas esperamos
 que en este caso te damos
 por abono la inocencia.

FRONDOSO: So much, in fact, that this fair maiden here,
Whom Heaven granted me as my dear bride,
And who gives me unbounded happiness,
Was kidnapped by Commander Don Fernán
Right from our wedding feast and taken to
His house as if she were his very own.
If she had not been able to defend
Herself and keep her virtue, as she did,
It's evident what would have happened there.

MENGO: And now is it not time for me to speak?
If you permit me, you will be amazed
To learn how he once treated me because
I tried hard to protect a girl of ours
When his men were about to kidnap her
And force her to his will most bestially.
That wicked Nero had me flogged until
My back was red and cut like salmon steaks.
Three men then drubbed my rear so lustily
That I believe I still could show the welts.
To heal my hide I had to spend more cash
On salves and poultices than on my farm!

ESTEBAN: Your Majesty, we want to be your folk.
You are our rightful king, and we have raised
Your royal coat of arms as proof of this.
We beg your clemency, and hope that you
Accept our word that we are innocent.

REY: Pues no puede averiguarse
el suceso por escrito,
aunque fué grave el delito,
por fuerza ha de perdonarse.
Y la villa es bien se quede
en mí, pues de mí se vale,
hasta ver si acaso sale
comendador que la herede.

FRONDOSO: Su majestad habla, en fin,
como quien tanto ha acertado.
Y aquí, discreto senado,
FUENTEOVEJUNA da fin.

KING: For lack of evidence about this case,
  Although a crime most grave, I am constrained
  To grant my royal pardon. And the town
  Is hereby placed beneath my own control,
  Since it has shown such loyalty to me,
  Until perhaps some good Commander may
  Come forth to rule with justice there some day.

FRONDOSO: Your Majesty has spoken, it is plain,
  Like one who has achieved so much for Spain.
  And here, dear audience, our interlude
  Named *Fuente Ovejuna* must conclude.